The Russian

Collector

The Russian

Collector

Lawrence Perlman

PRESS

Design by John Toren
Author Photograph by Sarah Rubinstein Photography

Forty Press, LLC
427 Van Buren Street
Anoka, MN 55303
www.fortypress.com

ISBN 978-1-938473-24-1

For Linda, a true muse

If we want things to stay
as they are, things will
have to change.

– *The Leopard*

Giuseppe Tomasi di Lampedusa

Prologue

Sofia Mostov watched the shiny black Rolls-Royce turn onto South Audley Street and come to a stop across from where she was standing. A black BMW pulled in close behind. Two stocky men in black suits got out of the BMW and walked to the front door of the restaurant to stand guard. The driver of the Rolls, wearing a chauffeur's cap, quickly opened the car's rear door and helped out a short, very obese man. He was soon followed by a tall woman with blonde hair wearing a mink coat. Another man of medium height wearing a gray suit and large glasses emerged from the passenger side of the car. It was the third time in the last five days she had watched this scene play out in front of the Japanese restaurant.

One of the men standing guard entered the restaurant, followed by the three Rolls passengers. The second guard turned for one last look around and then disappeared into the restaurant. Sofia Mostov thought to herself: *they follow the same procedure every time. Not good security. Too predictable.* She reached into her purse and tightened the suppressor onto her CZ100B pistol and confirmed that the safety was off.

She crossed the street and walked into the restaurant. The two men in black suits were already seated at their customary table next to the door where they could keep most of the long narrow room under observation. There were several tables in the front of the room and a long sushi bar on the right, beyond it was a row of banquettes on each wall. Sofia talked to the hostess who directed her to one of the seats at the sushi bar. The obese man, the tall blonde woman and the man in the grey suit were already seated at the banquette nearest the bar. Sofia's associates had told her that their seating habits never varied: same table, with the obese man on the banquette with his back to the wall, and the two others sitting on chairs facing him with the restaurant table between them.

The restaurant had clearly been expecting them. As soon as they sat down, a bottle of vodka in ice was brought, along with steaming bowls of miso soup and a large plate of noodles. Sofia had watched the three of them at lunch two days before. But they would not have recognized her. Two days ago she was an old woman, stooped and wearing a shapeless dress and a non-descript coat. Today she looked like she belonged at a high-end Mayfair restaurant. Her suit was clearly expensive, her shoulder bag had prominent LV monograms on each side, her blonde hair was perfectly coiffed and her fingernails painted a shade of blood red.

From her vantage point at the sushi bar, she watched them eat. The obese man didn't talk. He drank vodka between each mouthful of food; the first two courses supplemented by a plate of dumplings and two large rolls from the sushi bar. When he reached across the table to take food off the plates of his two companions, he spilled on his sweater and dipped a sleeve into a bowl of soy sauce. The woman walked around the table with a napkin to wipe off his sweater, but he brushed her hand aside and, speaking Russian loudly, told her to mind her own business. He held the nearly empty vodka bottle up and waved it until a flustered Japanese waitress brought him another. Sofia saw one of the sushi chefs roll his eyes.

As the meal progressed the obese man's head slowly drooped until his face lay in his bowl of noodles. He jerked his head up and loudly announced in Russian that he needed to pee. The man in the grey suit helped him up from the banquette and led him to the restrooms in the back of the restaurant. Sofia got up from her chair, took her purse and followed.

As she rounded the corner, she passed the man in the grey suit who was standing guard outside the door to the men's room. She smiled, but he didn't. She stopped at the door to the lady's room and rummaged through her purse. The man didn't turn. *Perfect*, she thought. She took out her pistol and fired two bullets into the back of his head. She caught his lifeless body, opened the door to the men's room, and pulled him in, propping his body against the door. She then walked through a second door and saw the obese man turning away from a urinal and struggling to zip up his pants. He staggered as he looked up at her, trying to focus his eyes. She fired two shots into his head, another into his heart.

She left the men's room, opened a utility closet that she had scouted out in her previous visit to the restaurant, and found the sign that said "closed for cleaning." She put it on the restroom door and walked out of the restaurant through a side door into an alley.

Sofia wiped the gun clean of fingerprints, threw it into a dumpster and walked into the bright London afternoon toward Hyde Park. She paused at a traffic light before crossing Park Lane. A man in a trench coat and brown hat strolled up next to her. As they waited for the light to change, she said to him in Russian "Your oligarch won't be giving the organization any more trouble. And you were right. He was a slob." The man grinned.

Chapter One

WISCONSIN

Fall was coming early to central Wisconsin. The rolling hills, the rich black farmland, and the mellowing forests seemed to be waiting peacefully for the inevitable winter. The maples that bordered the two-story white house on the edge of town were turning red, and the elms and oaks beyond were responding with yellow and gold. As she walked across the broad front porch, carrying a basket of late-summer raspberries, Catherine York reflected on her childhood home and how it was at the center of who she was.

The large kitchen in the old house had always been the place where the family gathered, and as she stood looking into it, an emotion of warm contentment swept over her. There was her mother, a few inches shorter than Catherine, grey hair pulled back in a bun, standing over the counter preparing dinner as she had so many times. It was as if nothing had changed, but she knew everything had.

She hadn't lived in the house for twenty-two years. She had gone off to Harvard at age eighteen, an adventure that took her to Cambridge and then to New York City where she had worked for many years as a senior executive in the large reinsurance firm of Larsen and McTabbitt. She now made more money than her parents, a retired postmaster and a retired school superintendent, could comprehend. And then there was Gerard.

"Oh, there you are dear," her mother said looking up from the roast she was chopping into small chunks for the stew she was preparing. "Well, you've collected a lot of berries there."

"There are a lot more bushes than I remember."

"They keep expanding."

"I bet you got those carrots and onions from your vegetable garden. I see Dad finally got around to building a fence around the garden to keep the animals out."

"Only this year." Her mother laughed.

"The backyard looks great—berry bushes, the apple trees, and some new flower gardens. It must keep you busy."

"I now have time to work out there, and your Dad helps. We never had time to work in the garden together. It's a nice experience."

"And my old swing is still there. I sat on it for a time. It brings back wonderful memories."

"Your dad keeps it there. He says for the grandchildren."

"You had better talk to your sons about that. I am not a very good prospect."

"We haven't given up on you." Her mother smiled. "But it pleases us so much that you are happy and so successful."

"Thanks." The old kitchen was silent. Then Catherine hugged her mother. "Mom, I'm so happy to be here with you and Dad and the boys. And you have been so welcoming to Gerard." Both women had tears in their eyes. "Let me help you with the chopping. I'll do the carrots."

They stood side-by-side in the kitchen. Catherine's mother said, "Have you unpacked?"

"Yes."

"Did you notice anything different about your room?"

"You repainted it!"

"Yes. We started to repaint it in the same white it was when you lived here. Then we decided to change the color. Do you like the blue?"

"I do. But blue walls or white, it's still my room."

"How does Gerard like the Badger Motel?"

"He says it is very comfortable."

"He could have stayed here. Your dad and I aren't prudes, and you are a grown woman."

"I know, Mom. But Gerard is a bit old-fashioned."

"Did I ever tell you about the first time your father and I spent the night together?"

"That would be way too much information!" They both laughed.

Catherine looked at the wall clock. "When do you expect them back?"

"Around five o'clock."

"It was nice of Dad and the boys to ask Gerard to go pheasant hunting with them."

"It was pretty impromptu. They started talking about hunting yesterday right after the two of you got here and just like that, they decided to go. I think it was Gerard's interest in joining them that led to the decision. They were surprised and probably a bit curious."

"Why do you say that?"

"He seems so—I don't know—sophisticated. I have trouble seeing him carrying a shotgun and tromping through a Wisconsin cornfield with the dogs."

"He loves bird hunting. His family owns an estate in Southern France where they are introducing pheasants."

"What is he really like? Has he ever been married? Does he have children?"

"No. But Mom, we are still getting to know each other. I can tell you that he is the most wonderful man I have ever met, except for Dad, of course.

"Of course."

"He is caring, sensitive and I feel safe with him. There is real passion between us. I have never had feelings for a man like I have for him. But he has lived alone, involved in the social and cultural life of Paris, for a long time. His work on big criminal cases challenges him. He seems to thrive on what he does, and the police force gives him a lot of autonomy. He likes the finer things in life—food, wine. He has more cashmere clothes than most clothing stores, but I have also seen him tough and resolute."

"Does he love you?"

"He says he loves me and I think I love him. But what does that mean after such a short time together?"

"Perhaps a lot."

"That he came here to meet all of you is a big thing."

"For a man, it's a very big step."

"He wants me to travel to France and meet his sister and her family. I think we have a future together. He believes the same thing. But we are still coming down from the high of the danger and excitement of the past months. I just don't know."

As Catherine's voice trailed off, her mother interrupted. "Catherine, you have always been so independent. I think that you stayed in that relationship with John so you could avoid commitment. You knew in your heart of hearts that you could never marry him. My sense is that this man is different. Mature. Strong. Comfortable in his own skin. But you are going to have to believe in your intuition. Take a leap."

Before Catherine could reply, they heard the door slam on Tommy's big truck. The back door to the kitchen opened and Catherine's father, two brothers and Gerard stood there smiling, each holding dead pheasants. Gerard was wearing a new blaze-orange cap featuring an American flag, a stained old hunting jacket borrowed from of one of the brothers and a pair of boots that showed the signs of a day in the field.

"Well, how was it?" Catherine's mother asked.

Tommy responded first, "We had a great time. Got our limit and gave a few more to the farmer. Kate, your man, Gerard, is a hell of a shot. He didn't miss one bird. The criminals of Paris must live in fear of him."

"Ah," said Gerard, "if only they were as easy to shoot as pheasants."

Everyone laughed, and then Tommy said, "And we had some great discussions. I asked Gerard how the two of you first met."

"And what did he tell you?"

"He told us a story that I can use to tease you in my delightful big brotherly way."

"Oh, he did?"

"Pardon," Gerard said in his rich French accent, "but I also told you that I noticed Catherine before we got to St. Barth. She caught my eye at the airport in St. Martin. Her beauty stood out even in that crowded place."

"Now Catherine, you are blushing," said her mother. "And since I am supposedly the only person in this family who doesn't know what happened on St. Barth, tell me now."

"Okay," said Catherine. "But Gerard should tell you."

Gerard began, "Earlier in the morning on the day in question—"

"'On the day in question'?" Catherine mocked. "Is this an interrogation?"

"—I had observed Catherine, who I recognized from the St. Martin airport, entering the jewelry store of Sofia Mostov. She stayed for quite a while. Later, I was having lunch at the Eden Roc restaurant, which is on a beautiful St. Barth beach, when I noticed Sofia Mostov on one of the beach lounge chairs. A short time later, Catherine arrived. It was as if Sofia was expecting her. They laid there briefly and then went swimming. I then left the restaurant. Naturally, I was suspicious of Catherine, since Sofia Mostov was a person of great interest to us in connection with a major criminal investigation. I visited Sofia Mostov's store the next day, and saw Catherine there again.

I got her name from a luggage tag at the airport, and when I was back in Paris, I had someone look her up and he reported back to me that she was an executive with a New York-based insurance company. I went to New York to meet with one of their senior executives, Mr. Nick Reschio. You can imagine my discomfort when he brought Catherine into the meeting. I requested a private meeting with Reschio to tell him about my suspicions regarding Catherine. After some awkwardness, we sorted things out, and Catherine and I worked on the case for the rest of the day."

"Gerard was gracious enough to apologize profusely," interjected Catherine. "And then on very short notice, he managed somehow to get a reservation at one of New York's finest restaurants and took me to dinner with Nick and his wife."

Catherine's mother said, "Quite a way to meet—thinking she was a criminal."

"Well," Gerard smiled, "she had a very dangerous look to her." Everyone laughed.

Tommy took the birds out back to clean them. Gerard said he would help. Catherine and her parents remained in the kitchen, the two women preparing dinner and Catherine's father sitting at the kitchen table.

"Dad, what did you guys talk about with Gerard other than me?"

"Well, we had a pretty good time. Gerard is an interesting fellow. A bit reserved, but I think he enjoyed the hunt. There was a lot of time to talk. We rested the dogs between hunts, had lunch and had time in the truck. He asked a lot of questions about my work as a school superintendent and about the boys' contracting business. We talked about the difference between the French and American school systems. Boy, they sure are tightly organized over there."

"Jack, quit eating all that bread," Catherine's mother interjected. "There won't be enough for dinner! Have a cookie if you are hungry."

Catherine laughed. *Some things never change,* she thought.

Jack York opened up the cookie jar and took four oatmeal

cookies out but put two back when he saw the disapproving look on his wife's face.

They talked a bit more about Gerard, Catherine's work, and about her upcoming trip to France.

Gerard and Tommy returned, and Tommy announced that the birds were in the freezer and that he was going to clean up for dinner. Gerard left for the motel but only after he looked admiringly at the large pot of beef stew on the stove.

"You are about to get a real down-home Wisconsin meal," said Catherine as she put her arms around Gerard.

"What is down-home?" said Gerard.

Tommy laughed and said, "You'll soon find out, but Mom's country stew is the best I've ever tasted."

Catherine's mother blushed and said, "All of you get out of here or you'll discover what goes into my secret recipe. Be back by six-thirty."

Then, the old kitchen was quiet and Catherine's mother said to her husband, "Catherine seems so happy."

"She does."

"This Gerard seems like the real deal."

"And he shoots darned well."

Chapter Two

MILAN

A heavy-set, dark-complexioned man with thick shiny black hair swept back into a pony tail walked into a restaurant not far from the Piazza del Duomo in Milan. Francesco Perez's face had high cheekbones and a prominent nose. His dark eyes surveyed the room until he saw a man sitting alone at a small round table in a corner of the crowded, simply furnished restaurant. He wore a black jacket with broad white stripes, grey slacks, and an open-collar white shirt. He was accompanied by a very broad-shouldered man with short blonde hair, wearing a black suit with an open collar white shirt. As Perez was being shown to his table, his companion took a seat at the bar with a view of the door and most of the restaurant.

Ettore Grassi rose to greet Perez. Of medium height, with a full head of grey hair and wearing horn-rimmed glasses, Grassi was dressed conservatively in a blue suit and striped tie. The two men hugged and sat down next to each other, both facing the front of the restaurant.

"I notice you brought a companion," said Grassi motioning to the bar in the front of the restaurant.

"Yes, they told me at the hotel that this was a very good restaurant, and I thought my friend might enjoy it. Are you here alone?"

"Of course. I have nothing to fear in Milan. Besides, the maître d' is my cousin and when I eat here the doorman only admits patrons who my cousin approves of. In Venice I don't need a companion. In Naples," and he frowned and gestured with his hand, "I don't dine alone."

"It is good to see you, Ettore. You look well and prosperous—like a banker, not a gangster," said Perez with a smile.

"Like you, Francesco, I'm a banker. And I hope you enjoy the restaurant. I want to repay you in a small way for the hospitality you showed me in Mexico City."

"It was a good meeting. I look forward to our partnership. I'm only sorry that our two dinners were at my villa. There are fine restaurants in Mexico City, but I find it safer and more relaxing to dine at the villa."

"Ah, yes, I assume you are referring to the traffic in Mexico City."

"Of course." The two men laughed and touched glasses of sparkling wine that Grassi had ordered.

Someone observing the Milan restaurant would have seen every table full, a well-dressed group of patrons in animated conversation, soft brown wainscoting and pale yellow walls all creating an atmosphere of relaxed elegance. At a round table in a corner, sat two men, their heads almost touching, as they cradled glasses of wine and talked.

"What we are going to do, Francesco, is not without risk, as we discussed in Mexico. Our friends in the South are not going to be happy about us engaging in business together. They will see it as upsetting a delicate balance."

"But," replied Francesco, "they have not exploited the opportunities in Italy. They could have expanded their market share and they have not. We have superior products, a very reliable source of supply and, working with you and your people, the means to achieve broad distribution. It's an opportunity that I don't want to pass up."

"I forgot that you're a graduate of Stanford Business School."

"I am. But they don't seem to consider me an example of how they would like to portray their graduates."

"Their problem."

"Well, I don't spend much time thinking about it, but I did learn at Stanford that the timid do not increase market share."

"I agree with you that broad distribution is important. And your concept of marketing heroin for as little as 50 Euros for a small dose of powder is very innovative. Users who are scared off by the fear of injecting the stuff can snort it or smoke it. A new market. We just have to be prepared for a bit of interference."

The two men then discussed the logistics of payment and how they would deal with allocating costs, splitting the profits and moving cash. Anyone overhearing the conversation would think that the two well-dressed and soft-spoken men were discussing a typical business deal.

"We have agreed that my organization will ship product in from Mexico through Marseilles and you will pick it up there and transport it by truck into Italy. Where will you break it down?" Francesco Perez asked, tipping his face close to Grassi.

"On the way to Genoa, there will be a detour into an area we call Liguria. Hilly, many small farms. Not many people. We have a place there where we will unpack the refrigerators, repackage the powder and move it into our distribution network."

"Then the now empty refrigerators will go on to Genoa."

"I am curious as to what you will do with all these excellent Mexican refrigerators once they have been—shall we say, unpacked."

"Francesco, you are having dinner with the CEO of one of the largest appliance distributors in Europe. You invoice us for the refrigerators, and we pay you in a conventional manner."

"Good. We generate such large amounts of cash that I am always looking for opportunities to process it. I recently purchased, for my colleagues, a horse-breeding operation in

LAWRENCE PERLMAN | 20

Kentucky in America. And I am Board Chair of a large Mexican appliance manufacturer. But I still don't know what you will do with the refrigerators. Dump them in the sea off of Genoa?"

"No. No. We clean them out. After all they have been on a long ocean voyage. Salt air and all that. Then we load them on a ship, take them on a nice trip around Italy and sell them as far north as Russia and as far east as Turkey. The next shipment might be resold in Spain or France. Your high-quality microwaves and stoves will follow the same routes. Some of the appliances will be shipped by truck as well. Genoa is a busy port—the movement of a couple of truckloads of appliances will go unnoticed."

"And you get to clean some money as well."

"Of course. We sell appliances at low prices, but make it up on volume."

"I remember that joke from business school, but you have come up with a way to make a big profit on the product and then make more money by selling the product's packaging. And we each get to clean some money on the appliance part of the transaction. Very, very good."

"Thank you. And, of course, our appliance business relationship is a fine cover for us."

"And—it is a wonderful excuse for this Mexican to come to Italy and enjoy your wonderful food and wine."

"Our next meeting should be in Venice. Very different cuisine and wines than that of Milan."

"I look forward to it," said Perez as he rose from the table and shook Grassi's hand. "The first shipment of refrigerators should arrive in Marseilles in about two days." With that, he motioned to the man at the bar and they both left the restaurant.

Chapter Three

After dinner, the York boys, their father, and Gerard sat on the front porch. In the growing dusk the only sounds were the crickets and the creaking of well-used rocking chairs.

Catherine stepped through the doorway, gently closing the screen door behind her. "You know, I thought nothing could improve on the smell of a fall evening in the country, but Gerard's Cuban cigars sure add to the aroma."

"Well, Kate, just think of it as one more burning leaf smell," said Tommy York, leaning back in his chair and taking a big draw from one of the H. Upmanns.

Catherine took a cigar from Gerard and settled on the front steps of the porch, her long legs extended on one step, her back resting against the railing.

"You look comfortable, dear," said her father. "That was always your favorite place to sit after dinner. It is good to have you home."

"Thanks, Dad. I remember those evenings. I felt safe and content." She thought to herself, *I have that feeling now.*

Catherine's father said, "Gerard, I am curious. Your English is very good, and so is your use of American colloquialisms. Where did you learn English?"

"Always the school superintendent," Catherine's mother teased her husband.

"He spent two years in the States as a French National

Police liaison to the FBI," Catherine said.

"Yes, those guys talked a lot in American sports idioms. I had to understand what they were saying or I would have missed the important parts," he laughed.

"So, you understood what Tommy said every time he missed a pheasant?" Bill smiled.

Gerard grinned, "He spoke an international language. The fellowship of missed shots. All of us who shoot know that language very well." Everyone laughed. He continued in a more serious tone. "But I first learned English from my father, who spent four years in England during the war." Gerard's cigar burned a bit brighter.

The three York men leaned forward a bit, intrigued by Gerard's comments.

"He was an officer in the French army, and was part of a group of young officers who warned about how ill prepared the French were for what they thought was an inevitable war with Germany. After France surrendered in 1940, he joined de Gaulle in England, worked with the British and the Americans and then fought alongside the Americans in Europe. He was impressed with the vigor and economic strength of America and invested in American companies after the war."

"He also bought a lot of work by soon-to-be important American painters," Catherine added.

"Yes, he did. Catherine has seen much of his collection. He had a good eye. He would have adored Catherine." Catherine flicked her cigar ash toward Gerard. "So, when I was quite young he began to teach me English and I kept studying it in school."

"Your dad was an investor?" asked Catherine's mother.

"He was, but we also had a lot of real estate in France. Much of it in Southern France. My sister now lives with her family on one of our estates not too far from Avignon. I inherited the family apartment in Paris."

"With all the advantages you had growing up, why become

a policeman?" Catherine's mother asked. "What did your parents think of your decision?"

"Let me respond to your second question first. My father encouraged me to join the French National Police and in a moment I will tell you why. But, after I graduated from the university I took the same route followed by many of my classmates, and went to work with the French government. The Ministry I joined was involved in national security matters, and I found that I liked complex investigations and apparently had some aptitude for them.

"My father and I talked about my career, and he opened up to me in ways he never had. He wasn't much for revealing his feelings or, for that matter, showing affection or giving compliments. Like many of his generation, he was scarred and shamed by the French Army surrender to the Germans and then by the extent the French authorities collaborated with the German occupiers. Some of his strongest contempt was directed at the French police who turned on their Jewish neighbors and deported them to death camps and who hunted Resistance fighters.

"After the war, he advocated for a stronger, more professional police force that would be independent and not so subject to political influence. He told me that the best way for me to serve the country would either be in the military or the police. He much favored the police and said that because I would be independently wealthy that I had a special obligation to serve.

"One of his colleagues from the army was a senior official in the National Police. I met with him and he told me that the skills in investigation I had demonstrated in the Ministry would suit me for police work and encouraged me to join the force. He said that I could be part of an important transformation that could make a real difference for France: the creation of a professional police organization that would be independent of politics. One that could protect all the French people.

"I was at a crossroads. I had never thought of myself as having a responsibility to serve the country. I never before had thought that possessing independent wealth carried with it an obligation. But, I didn't want to become a bureaucrat—I had always been a bit of an adventurer and somewhat of a loner.

"I took leave of the Ministry that fall to think about what I wanted to do with my life. I traveled, did some mountain climbing, spent the winter skiing, and then came back in the spring and became a cop. I went through training, paid my dues on the street and then was assigned as a liaison to the Army Intelligence Service. From there, I started to work somewhat independently on a variety of cases, and I resisted the opportunities to progress on the administration side of the force. I liked my independence and I liked working on hard cases. And that is how I became a cop."

"I thought it was because you just like to shoot people," said Catherine.

Gerard laughed and said, "Well, my mother was never too happy about my career choice. She said that she worried about my father every day during the war and now she worried about her son every day when he went off to his job. But to her, it was important that my decision was so strongly supported by my father. Shortly before he died, I received a commendation for investigating a series of armed robberies. At the commendation ceremony, my father told me how proud of me he was and how important my work was. His comment has always meant a great deal to me."

"Well, it's getting late," said Catherine's father, and my cigar, as big as it was, is pretty much gone."

"I will drive Gerard back to the motel. See you all in the morning," said Catherine.

"Again, thank you for a wonderful evening," said Gerard.

As everyone rose from the porch, there were handshakes and hugging.

In the car, Catherine said to Gerard, "You were quite a hit with my family."

"Catherine, they are good and genuine people. No pretensions. I felt very comfortable with them. As, increasingly, I do with you. I can only hope that you and your family feel the same way about me."

"Oh, quit fishing for a compliment. They do like you. Oh, and so do I," she said, reaching one hand from the steering wheel and putting it on his thigh.

As they walked into his motel room, Gerard said, "Thank you for driving me back to the motel, but before you leave I have a question. Why is this called the Badger Motel?"

Catherine replied, "A lot of things in Wisconsin are named after badgers. The badger is the state animal. This is the badger state."

"American states have state animals?"

"Sure, we also have state flowers and some states have state foods."

"But why a badger?"

"You'd think lions or tigers would be more dramatic, I suppose, but there aren't any in Wisconsin."

"Okay, but there are bears here."

"Gerard, all I know is that it is badgers. Minnesota, the state next door, is the gopher state. Gophers are their state animal."

"What is a gopher?"

"It's a prairie rodent."

"The state animal is a rodent?"

"Sure. This is America. We love animals—apparently all kinds."

They both laughed and Catherine asked him how he enjoyed the day.

"It was wonderful. Your brothers and father are fine men. I have never hunted in a cornfield before. It was beautiful—the golden color of the cornstalks, the blue sky, the dogs working."

"You sure scuffed up those beautiful boots."

"Ah, yes, but they are French boots—JW Weston—and Weston will restore them for me. I have had these boots for many years."

"Did you like my mom's stew?"

"Your mother's stew was delicious, as was her apple pie. I haven't had apple pie since I lived in Washington, D.C."

"You don't have apple pie in France?"

"We have something we call tarte tatin—but it is different and we drink sauterne with it—not milk. And we normally don't serve it with cheese—that was a treat."

"Well, we don't have the varieties of cheese that you do in France, but Wisconsin cheddar is pretty darned good."

"Catherine, two days here and you are starting to talk like your family."

"I am tempted to respond with, *you betcha*, but I won't." They both laughed.

"I'm so glad you came," she said.

"It was important to me to come here, to meet your family, to understand you better."

"And to experience drinking wine out of a box," Catherine teased.

"Well, I admit I was confused. I first thought that your mother was serving milk with the beef stew."

"The look on your face when my dad asked if you would like wine, and then started to pour from the carton, was priceless."

"It was a new experience, I admit. In France, wine comes in bottles."

Catherine smiled. "Oh yes, Mr. Voyeur, there is something else. You left something out of the story of how we met."

"Well, I am discrete, am I not?" Gerard said as he took her in his arms. "I could not tell your family that on the beach at St. Barth, Sofia proceeded to apply suntan lotion to your back and in the process removed the top part of your bathing suit like this," Gerard said as he lifted her shirt and unclasped her bra. "And that she then turned you over on your back as she applied lotion to your front, like this."

"Ah," Catherine said, smiling, "it's all coming back now." And she reached up and kissed him as he gently lowered her onto the bed.

Chapter Four

Four men, two Mexicans and two Italians, sat at a table in a café abutting the historic old Marseilles harbor. On a sunny afternoon, fishing boats made their way through the crowded waters unloading their catches near the harbor's fish mongers who worked behind old metal tables, scarred from thousands of knife strokes.

One of the men, a tall Italian in his forties with close-cropped grey hair, was talking on a cell phone. When he finished, he put the phone down, and said, "The ship is on schedule. It will dock at the port early tomorrow morning. He will arrange for our containers to be among the first to be unloaded."

"Stefano, are you sure that you can trust this customs inspector?" asked a man of medium height, with dark hair and muscular forearms, speaking Italian somewhat awkwardly with a strong Spanish accent.

"Well, Marcos, when I was here two weeks ago, I gave him an envelope fat with Euros. If things go as planned, he will get another envelope tomorrow. And he certainly knows the port routine."

Marcos gritted his teeth, "If he values his health he will do what he is paid to do and keep his mouth shut."

The second Mexican, Luis, who had been sitting quietly, said "Easy, Marcos, enjoy this beautiful afternoon. I am confident that Stefano knows what he is doing and that the customs inspector will be able to go home to his family tomorrow night and forget to tell his wife about his extra money. Now, try to look natural. Perez said that we shouldn't stand out."

"I am blending in—I am wearing this French golf shirt with an alligator on it," said Marcos.

"It is a crocodile," said Luis, "but how would you know what a golf shirt even looked like?"

Marcos replied defensively, "The guy at the souk told me it was a well-known French golf shirt."

"You take the word of a street vendor who is selling you a false shirt—a knock-off?" laughed Luis. "Besides, you could wear a beret, and with that dark complexion, jet black hair, and your broken nose, you would still look like you just got off a Mexico City bus."

"Luis, the shirt cost me forty Euros. It must be real."

"If it was real the alligator on the chest wouldn't be crooked."

"*Adesso basta,*" said another of the four, short and wiry, and wearing a large mustache. Then switching from Italian to Spanish, Vinello said, "Relax and look at the pretty girls. We will be busy enough tomorrow. We probably shouldn't even be out here."

"The less time in that hotel in Le Canut full of smelly, drunken sailors," said Luis. "Look at that table near the water—now those women are good looking."

"Probably off one of the cruise ships. They will sit here, do a lot of shopping and giggle at all the Arab men staring at them," said Vinello. "Dressed like that, they better take a taxi to their ship. There are neighborhoods they should stay out of."

Stefano got up from the table and said "I am going to take a walk and dispose of this cell phone. Maybe I will buy one of those crocodile shirts." Marcos looked embarrassed as the others laughed.

A while later, as the Italian returned to the table, his partner Vinello said, "Stefano, no shirt?"

"No shirt." Then speaking slowly in Spanish, he said, "But I walked up there," pointing to one of the beautiful old churches on the hill, "to get a better view, because I saw an orange Volvo parked on one of the streets leading to the harbor."

"Why did you notice an orange Volvo?" asked Luis.

Vinello twirled the ends of his mustache and said, "Stefano notices everything. He was once a cop, but he decided he could make more money working with us than living off of—how would you say it in Spanish—*corruziones.*"

"*Saborno. Saborno.* So why the orange Volvo?" asked Marcos.

"Because it followed us to Marseilles yesterday."

"All the way from Milan?"

"I don't know. I didn't notice it until we got near Nice. Then I realized that I had seen it while we were still in Italy. It has Naples plates."

"*Maldetto,*" said Vinnello in rapid Italian. "The southerners may have gotten wind of what we are up to. That could be very bad—particularly if they see us unloading the crates from the ship."

Luis interjected, "We know how to handle problems, do we not, Marcos?"

"*Si*—direct action—always direct action," said Marcos. "*A falta de caractere!*—failure to act shows weakness—that is our way. And that is our instruction from Perez."

"If we don't see them today," said Luis, "Marcos and I should be able to spot them tomorrow if they are watching the dockyard."

Stefano, looking around carefully, said, "Here is a map of the port. You see on the south side, there is a hill that overlooks the location where the customs inspector says the containers will be unloaded. You two position yourselves up on the hill. You will have a good view of the transfer, and if you sense a problem, call us on this cell phone." He pushed a phone across the table. "When Vinello and I leave with the trucks, go back to Paris and be careful. We will be in touch soon."

"Our boss met with your Francesco Perez in Milan last week. If tomorrow's transfer is successful, we will be seeing a lot of each other."

"Any suggestions of where Marcos and I can dine tonight?" asked Luis.

"I don't think you will find tacos in Marseilles, but there are some small restaurants not too far from your hotel where you can find good local food. Marseilles is famous for fish stew called bouillabaisse. Another fish stew that I think is more interesting is called bourride, made with shrimp and cod or turbot, served with aioli. It usually has a lot of garlic and saffron, so try it with a local flavorful rosé."

"Well, thank you Stefano. I wouldn't have taken you for a gourmet."

"I am not a gourmet. I am an Italian."

♦ ♦ ♦

The next morning in a remote corner of the huge industrial harbor, the Italians, Stefano and Vinello watched as dockworkers used forklifts to load crates marked, *Frigorifico Producto de Mexico,* onto two large white trucks, bearing Italian license plates. A man wearing the uniform of a French customs inspector drove up in a four-wheel utility vehicle bearing the seal of the Port of Marseilles.

Vinello joined two Italian truck drivers and supervised the loading of the crates onto the trucks. Stefano went to speak to the customs officer.

"Any problems?" Stefano asked.

"No, no. My men opened one crate, saw a refrigerator and signed the inspection report."

"Good. Here is the second half of our contribution to the customs officers' retirement fund," he said as he handed the man a large well-stuffed envelope.

On the heights that overlooked the dockyard, next to a small deserted parking area, Marcos and Luis were crouching behind a low wall, their backs to the port, watching two men who stood next to an orange Volvo, one peering at the dockyard through binoculars and the other photographing it with an Olympus camera equipped with a large telephoto lens.

Luis whispered instructions to Marcos. Moments later, he saw Marcos quietly come up behind the man with the binoculars, grab his head, put his knee in his back and pull his head back until it cracked. As the camera man turned to see what the noise was, Luis got to his knees, rested his Nighthawk Custom Predator Enforcer .45 caliber semi-automatic on the wall and fired a shot into the man's chest. The sound of the powerful pistol was muted by the suppressor attached to the barrel.

As Marcos quickly removed the memory card from the Olympus, Luis fired one more bullet into the head of each of the men now lying on the hard pavement of the parking lot.

After tossing the pistol over the wall into a weedy patch, the two Mexicans boarded a bus to the St. Charles rail station where they disposed of their gloves and bought tickets on the bullet train to Paris. Three hours later they were in Paris and an hour after that, they were eating heartily at a restaurant on the Rue Amelot in the Third Arrondissement that served Mexican dishes and where the waiters spoke Spanish.

The two trucks had long made their way out of Marseilles and were now moving past Monaco and into Italy.

Chapter Five

MARSEILLES

Two Marseilles officers, standing on a hill overlooking the port, were inspecting the crime scene where the two Italians had been killed, when Pierre Abou arrived.

"So you came alone, Abou?" said a heavyset detective wearing a trench coat. "Where is the famous detective, de Rochenoir?"

"He will be here shortly, Inspector Monsey. But I am accompanied by a Department consultant."

"Okay, where is this consultant?"

"He's here with me. His name is Sherlock Holmes."

"Ah, yes. I'm glad you're still studying Sherlock Holmes. Anything to improve your investigation skills."

"And I see you are wearing the same coat you had when I left Marseilles for Paris five years ago. I recognize the stains."

"As I recall, Pierre, you were a master of stains. Do you still use your neckties as napkins?"

Pierre smiled and made an elaborate motion of tightening the knot of his tie.

"But enough of these pleasantries," continued Monsey. "Let me tell you what happened so you can go back to Paris and we can complete this investigation."

Abou interrupted, "Maurice, just a moment. I see that Senior Inspector de Rochenoir has arrived."

After greeting Gerard, Inspector Monsey of the Marseilles

police said, "Senior Inspector, I was just about to tell Abou what happened here. I wouldn't want to detain you. I am sure you have more important cases to work on than a couple of low-life murders so far from Paris."

Gerard nodded with a smile. "I would be most grateful to hear what you have discovered, Inspector."

Monsey shifted uneasily on his feet.

"Well, two unfortunate Italians, who are now resting at our morgue, were both shot—one twice, the other once. They must have been observing something at the dockyards down there. We found a camera and a pair of binoculars by their bodies. Their identification cards and driver's licenses show they are from Naples. We called the Naples police and they said these guys were low level mobsters—part of the Camorra. We are not sure what they were doing here. Maybe some kind of meeting. But they were certainly killed by one of our local thugs. Our homegrown gangsters are very protective of their turf being invaded by Italians, Russians or others who occasionally want to get involved in our beautiful city."

"Have you found a weapon or cartridge casings?"

"Yes, Senior Inspector. Three casings, and we just found a handgun in the weeds over there. We expect it to be the killer's." He held out two plastic bags to Gerard, who pointed to Pierre.

Monsey handed the bags to Pierre. One contained three shell casings and the other a large semi-automatic pistol. Monsey commented, "We haven't seen one of these guns around here. Our bad guys usually favor Berettas."

Pierre put on white gloves and examined the casings and the gun. "The gun is a .45 and the casing is a .45."

Pierre and Gerard looked at where the bodies had fallen, walked around the orange Volvo and examined the binoculars and the Olympus camera. They walked behind the low wall on the hill and looked down at the port. Gerard turned to Monsey, "We would like to see the bodies."

"Okay, but the examiner hasn't gotten to the bodies yet."

Pierre said, "We will handle them with the respect and delicacy they deserve."

The Marseilles morgue, a dark gloomy place located in a rundown neighborhood not far from the dockyards, smelled of formaldehyde and mold. Walking through the dark hallways, covered with peeling paint, Pierre thought to himself, *probably the way the old Paris morgue smelled.*

Wearing surgical masks and gloves, Gerard and Pierre examined the two bodies, using a magnifying glass and a small flashlight. They talked for a few minutes and then asked to be driven back to the crime scene so they could take photos of the pavement where the heads of the two victims had landed.

Pierre requested to see the shipping records of the dockyard for the day of the murders.

Monsey said, "Abou, do you think the shooter escaped on a ship?"

"I will let you know tomorrow. Now I am going to have dinner with my parents, and Gerard is going to get some rest. It's a long trip from Wisconsin."

"Say hello to your parents and tell your father to do something about the price of fish. It is becoming too expensive for a cop's salary."

Pierre shrugged his shoulders and said, "My father is not getting rich, so maybe you ought to arrest the middlemen."

◆　◆　◆

Sitting in a taxi on his way to the meeting the next morning, Pierre Abou reflected on his breakfast conversation with Gerard. Asked what theory the Marseilles police had, Pierre replied that they considered it to be an action taken by the Marseilles underworld to protect their turf. Gerard asked if he agreed with that conclusion. Pierre said he did initially, but that as he considered his observations, he had grown increasingly skeptical.

Gerard said, "I think we can get some help from your friend, Sherlock Holmes."

Pierre smiled and said, "Okay, Gerard, tell me what Holmes can offer us."

"Pierre, you will remember the Holmes's story called, *The Adventures of the Speckled Band.*"

"Yes."

"Then you will recall that what is important to this investigation is that Holmes admits to Watson that he had reached the wrong conclusion. He said something like, 'it is dangerous to reason from insufficient data.' That's what I believe the Marseilles police have done. You told me that Monsey was viewed as lazy when you were on the Marseilles force."

"I doubt he has changed much."

"Well, I don't think the facts lead to their conclusion that the assailants are from Marseilles." He then went on to explain his reasoning to Pierre, who affirmed his conclusion.

The taxi stopped in front of the Marseilles Police Headquarters. Pierre walked to a small windowless conference room he remembered so well. Three Marseilles detectives looked up impatiently.

"Well, Abou," said Monsey, "did the National Police solve the crime for us overnight?"

"You know, Maurice, if I didn't know how collaborative you are, I would think you didn't want me here. And I was going to bring you some fish as a goodbye present. But now you will have to do with some conclusions from Sherlock Holmes and me as well as Gerard, who will be here shortly."

The four men engaged in light talk until, thirty minutes later, Gerard entered the room.

Monsey said, "Come on, gentlemen, we don't have the whole morning."

Without acknowledging Monsey's comment, Gerard began, "My apologies, gentleman. I was late for this meeting because I had to pick up some enlargements of the photos of the crime scene that Pierre took yesterday." He set them on the table. "I will start with the bodies of the victims. While I know that your medical examiner has not yet begun his work, I think he will find that victim number one," and he pointed to a diagram of the crime scene identifying where the bodies were found, "died not from a gunshot wound but from a broken neck."

"But he was shot in the head," interrupted one of the detectives.

"Yes, he was. But I think his neck was first broken, and I believe he was shot after he had fallen to the ground dead."

"I don't know what difference it makes," said Monsey. "Dead is dead."

"He was shot in the back of the head," responded Pierre, "and the bullet was found almost under his face. The bullet was deformed in a way that only could have resulted from it striking a hard surface like the parking lot pavement after it exited the victim's head.

Looking directly at Monsey, Gerard said, "And though your people prematurely cleaned up the scene, the notes of the officer who did the cleaning refer to brain fragments on the pavement under the victim's face. I also noticed the residue of brain fragments on his face when I examined the body. A bullet fired at close range that hits a hard surface like the pavement after exiting the victim will be flattened, as is the case with this bullet. So, it's likely that he was shot while lying on the ground."

I will explain in a moment why the condition of the bullet is important, but let me go on." Pointing to their photographs, Gerard said, "Do you see the differences in the entrance wounds of the two victims?"

One of the detectives, staring at the photos, said, "It looks like one was shot in the front of the head, the other in the back of his head. But the guy who was shot in the front was also shot through the heart."

"You have a future in police work, my young friend. You should come to Paris."

Monsey sneered. "Why should we care about where on their bodies the bullets entered?"

"I care, Inspector Monsey, and you should too," said Gerard. "Your detective was describing the wounds on victim number two. The shot through the heart was clean—the shooter was good—and it would have killed victim number two immediately. He most likely fell backwards and was subsequently shot through his forehead after he was dead, just like victim number one. Oh, and I found brain matter matted in the back of his hair. And the bullet showed the same deformity—consistent with hitting the pavement—as the bullet that went through the first victim's head.

"Now look at this photo. It shows the three bullets recovered from the scene. The one I have numbered 'C' was found by your men perhaps fifty meters from the crime scene in a weed patch, and it's barely deformed. I'm certain that the ballistics test will show that it's from the same gun as the other two bullets. The heart shot was probably fired from behind the stone wall where the casing was found, and the bullet traveled through the victim's body before landing in the weed patch.

"From all this, I surmise that there were two killers. One killed victim number one by breaking his neck. The other one shot victim number two in the heart from behind the wall, and then probably walked over and shot each one through the head. The shooter was not leaving anything to chance. If the area around the victim's Volvo had not been cleaned up by your diligent cops, we might even have found footprints left by the killers."

The three Marseilles detectives stared at Gerard, his diagram and the photos. Before they could say anything, Pierre went on. "Then there is the matter of the memory card from the Olympus camera that was found on the ground at the scene, bearing the fingerprints of victim number one."

"Wait a minute, Abou. There wasn't a memory card in the camera."

"Exactly. While my consultant, Mister Holmes, was working a case and talking to the local police inspector, he referred to a 'curious incident' involving a dog who was at the scene of the crime. He said something like, *The dog, a watchdog, did nothing in the night.* The inspector questioned why he was bringing that up and Holmes replied, *The dog was a watchdog, yet he did not bark. That was the 'curious incident.'* The silence of the watchdog led Holmes to the conclusion that the perpetrator of the crime in question must have known the dog well."

"What's your point, Abou?" said a frutstrated Monsey.

"Don't you think it strange that these guys were taking pictures without a memory card in the camera? So, whatever they were photographing, the killers did not want the pictures found. That is why there is no memory card. That is the curious incident. The killers took the memory card."

Monsey fidgeted uncomfortably in his chair.

"Pierre," said Gerard, "explain to our friends the significance of the weapon that was found at the crime scene."

"It was found on the hill below the crime scene, probably discarded by the killer who did not want to risk carrying it. It is a .45-caliber Nighthawk Enforcer.

"Have you seen that model in Marseilles?" asked Gerard.

Three heads shook 'no' in unison.

"I didn't think so. Pierre, please continue."

"It's an expensive gun. It has a relatively long barrel, so it has good range for a handgun, shoots a .45-caliber bullet, and can accommodate very sophisticated sights as well as a suppressor."

"Too expensive for the military, or under-equipped cops, but a perfect gun for bad guys who need a pistol that can fire a powerful bullet quietly with accuracy," Gerard said.

"I have only seen a gun of this type once before," added Pierre, "and that was last year, in Paris, when we examined the gun safe ear of a Mexican drug bigwig. He had two."

"I called our firearms expert this morning," said Gerard. "He told me that model is often used by Mexican and Russian drug cartels."

"And you will recall that I checked the shipping records of the port yesterday afternoon," said Pierre. "A freighter that carried refrigerators from Mexico was unloaded yesterday."

"Okay, Abou and Senior Inspector de Rochenoir, you have identified a lot of facts—but so what? Where do we go from here?" asked Monsey, his face flushed.

Sitting back in his chair, Gerard stroked his chin and said, "These murders were particularly violent. It was as if a message was being delivered. Drug cartels such as the Mexicans and the Russians are brutal—they believe in the effectiveness of direct action. Pierre has pointed out to me that Marseilles thugs tend to defend their turf with beatings and other forms of intimidation, but rarely murders. And your inquiries through your contacts have turned up nothing except denials that the locals were involved. Now why would they be photographing the dockyards? Is it just a coincidence that the weapon used is a favorite of the Mexicans and that part of the cargo unloaded was from Mexico?

"It's possible, of course, that this crime was committed by locals defending their territory, but I think it is more likely that there is much more to it. I suggest that you canvas local hotels and see if anyone with Mexican passports stayed in Marseilles the night before the murders. And, of course, continue to press the local gangs—they may know something.

"Please send me the results of the medical examiner's work and I will send you a copy of our report."

Monsey slumped slightly.

"Don't worry, Maurice," said Gerard, "our report will applaud the careful work of your team." Then, as he got up from the table to leave, Pierre added. "Our consultant, Mr. Holmes, is leaving with us, but he would want me to remind you of the danger of reasoning from insufficient data."

Chapter Six

Marcos and Luis climbed the stairs out of the Boulainvilliers metro station and walked into the growing Paris darkness. An elderly couple walking a small white dog approached the two Mexicans on the sidewalk. As the couple got closer they suddenly turned and hurried across the street. Once on the other side, they continued to walk very fast, while frequently looking over their shoulders. Marcos said, "What are they afraid of, that we will steal that ridiculous little dog?"

They turned the corner. "Perez likes big houses with tall walls," Marcos said.

"And wealthy neighborhoods," Luis responded. "His villa outside of Mexico City has big gardens." Reaching a large three-story brick and stone house, Luis stopped, looked around and said, "Here it is, close to the Bois de Boulogne. We need to take this pathway around to the back of the house."

They approached a sturdy wooden gate set in a brick wall and, after waving at a security camera, pressed a button on an intercom and were buzzed into the rear courtyard.

"I wonder who gets to use the front entrance?"

"I don't know," said Luis, "but ever since the French police searched his house in connection with that jewelry caper, Perez has been worried that the French have him under surveillance, so he doesn't want to be seen with us."

"We could come in disguised as gardeners. Then no one

would notice us."

"Marcos, you have a point. Sort of like the invisible Mexicans in California. There must be rich Anglo kids there who think that all Mexicans are gardeners."

Marcos smiled as the door to the house opened. A stocky broad-shouldered man with short blond hair, wearing black jeans and a tight white t-shirt, filled the doorway.

"Hello Diego," Luis smiled. "I'm glad that Perez brought his security with him on this trip. You pack, even in the house." He pointed to a Glock 17 in Diego's shoulder holster.

"I heard you were coming over." And then he hugged the visitors. "Good to see you; I hear you have been busy."

"And you are still lifting weights—your muscles now have muscles," said Marcos.

"You are two tough looking hombres," Diego said. "You will scare our neighbors."

"I think we already have," said Luis.

"The boss is waiting for you in the study. I will take you there, but so you are not surprised, we flew in with El Gordo. He's with the boss."

"I thought he never left Mexico, with the Americans and everyone else after him."

"I think he was getting frustrated always moving from one place to another. Like the boss, he says he loves Paris and misses it. We picked him up in Caracas. He used a Venezuelan passport at the Paris airport—they barely looked at him. Maybe the Gulfstream impressed the border police.

"He changed his appearance a bit for this trip. Wore a hairpiece. Looked like a mop. But if you even mention his hairpiece to anyone, I will break both your necks." Marcos and Luis looked at each other. "He said on the plane that he wanted to spend a few days here. Even took a walk on the Champs-Élysées, had some suits made, and ate at a fancy restaurant."

"Did Perez go with him?"

"Hell no! He doesn't think El Gordo should even be in

Paris. He's worried that someone will notice him."

"Unlikely. Very few people have seen him in recent years. I have never seen him. Have you seen him, Marcos?" Marcos shook his head no.

"Okay, here is the study. Be careful. These guys are working on some big things. Good to see you."

The two Mexicans entered a large room with walls paneled in dark wood, thick Persian rugs on the parquet floor and heavy drapes drawn over the windows. Large, colorful paintings were on two of the walls of the room. There were bookcases on one wall and a large globe in a corner. In the center of the room was a large, leather couch flanked by an armchair in a rose-colored fabric that picked up a color from the Persian rug.

A large man with a pointed, bald head that Luis thought resembled a cannon shell sat on the couch. He wore a loose-fitting leisure suit and his jowls looked to Luis like they hung on his face. His heavy eyelids almost covered his eyes.

Luis and Marcos stared at the man who was their ultimate boss, the head of one of the largest drug cartels in Mexico.

Perez broke the silence. "It's impolite, hombres, to stare. My guest is only here for a few days and his presence should tell you how important the work you are doing is to the organization. But first I want to congratulate you on how you dealt with the situation in Marseilles. You did exactly what you should have at the port. If things continue to go well, your families will be living in larger houses.

"One of the reasons you are here this evening is so we can explain to you our plans for this operation with the Italians. By understanding the big picture you can figure out a solution to the inevitable unexpected problems that will come up. That is what you did in Marseilles, and it's why we are trusting you with a related matter."

Suddenly, a deep gravelly voice came out of the previously passive figure on the couch. Marcos almost jumped when he heard it. The voice was unmistakable—the two had heard it in recorded messages numerous times.

"Our product is the best in the world," he said. "The demand for it is insatiable. We need new markets. Northern Italy is the first step in expanding into Europe—particularly Eastern Europe. Huge markets, cooperative authorities. We have formed an alliance with a Northern Italian family as you know. The groups in the south of Italy have somehow gotten wind of our partnership. They were spying on the refrigerator delivery in the Marseilles port. But we must take action now to make it clear to the southerners that they are not to meddle in our business. That is your task. Our partners have some leaks—their code of silence seems not to be as strong as ours—perhaps because their enforcement is not as swift and harsh as ours."

"We can't count on our Italian partners to deliver the message with sufficient—shall I say—impact to the southerners. Indeed, once we have control of our partner's distribution system we will have little use for them. The people we are forming a relationship with in the South will be more important to us, for a while."

"I'm sending Gilberto to Naples to work with you there and in France. He is a good man and speaks both Italian and French. The three of you and some other assets—both Italian and Mexican—that we have in Naples are to cauterize the wound and deliver the message our way. Francesco will go into the details."

Luis and Marcos remained standing. They had not taken their eyes off El Gordo during his monologue. When he was finished, he returned to his impassive state. During his comments only his eyes and his mouth moved, not even gesturing with his arms. Even Perez had watched him intensely.

Perez stood and looked at Marcos and Luis. "You are to go to Naples and meet up with Gilberto and our people there. Two of whom you know. We think we know who ordered the surveillance of the Marseilles port. Some southerners think the surveillance was an unwise move. They won't do anything about it, but they won't interfere with us if we take action. They are waiting to decide if they will join us. We need to make it clear to them what the consequences are for opposing us. We will link up with another family if they don't make a decision fast."

Handing Luis an envelope and a cell phone, he said, "Here are your travel plans along with many Euros. After the next shipment is delivered, go to Naples. Luis, you will be called on this phone with meeting details. We already have some allies down there who you will meet. We have been assured that they are reliable and greedy. Greed can be an asset if as long as once they are bought they stay bought. There are weapons already in place, including some very sharp knives."

"Thank you," said Luis.

"Diego will show you out. Take him to dinner. He needs a change of scenery."

Chapter Seven

The next morning, Catherine worked out in the gym of her apartment building and, with her dress pumps in her shoulder bag, took a deep breath of the New York autumn morning and walked to the Larson and McTabbitt headquarters on Park Avenue, just north of Grand Central station. Shortly after she settled in, her boss, Nick Reschio, stood at the doorway to her office.

Catherine liked working for Nick Reschio. Five-foot ten with blond hair turning to gray, Reschio still had the strong shoulders and neck of a former wrestler and linebacker at Williams. An Executive Vice-President of Larson and McTabbitt, he was one of the top five executives in the firm.

"Kate, it's good to have you back. We have missed our ace investigator. Later, I want to hear how Gerard's visit to Wisconsin went, but for now we have a problem that is right up your alley. We have a coverage application that looks fishy to me. Take a quick look at this file. Can you come to my office this afternoon after lunch?"

"Sure."

After a lunch at her desk, Catherine walked into Nick Reschio's office. He was on his phone and signaled her to sit down. She sat down at his conference table while he finished the conversation.

His office always reminded Catherine of a men's club with its dark wood and leather. A Marine Corps sword was prominently displayed in a glass case, a memento of the five years Reschio had spent as a Marine officer between college and Harvard Business School. The walls were bare, except for a few sailing scenes carefully selected by his assistant from the L&M Collection. Nick hardly noticed them. His only interest in water was to drink it one ice cube at a time with single malt scotch.

Nick ended his conversation and sat down next to her at the table. "Well, Kate. What do you think?"

"I didn't have much time to look at the files, but we are being asked to take a big piece of coverage on six very valuable paintings surrounded by a lot of red flags."

"You know a lot more about art than I do, but the application looks pretty thin for an estimated value north of two-hundred million. Are these paintings that valuable?"

"Except for one Picasso, these are all works from the late nineteenth century, and the artists are famous impressionists—Renoir, Pissarro, Cézanne, Cassatt. With two huge ifs, these valuations seem in the ballpark."

"And the 'ifs' are?"

"Are they the real thing and do the owners have an insurable interest?"

"Provenance?"

"Sketchy. None of them came out of an auction house."

"Why is that important?"

Catherine opened the file and pointed to the list of paintings. "Because an auction house would have done some work to determine authenticity. It would give us something to go on. If we accept, we will have to do various tests, have experts look at them to validate their legitimacy, and insist on more detailed provenance. I have done a quick search on the Cézanne. If it is the painting I think it is, it disappeared during the war and hasn't turned up. The Nazis seized it from a

French dealer who was later killed. There is a bill of sale for it in the file, from the dealer to someone with a German name, at a ridiculously low price. The next piece of provenance is a reference to what could be this painting on a list of works the Russians brought back to the USSR at the end of the war. Then there is a copy of what is probably a decree and some legislation from the Russians claiming as property of the USSR, all art taken from the Germans. There is what appears to be a receipt from some agency of the Russian Government in rubles."

"The Renoir?" Nick asked.

"Authentication by a German dealer, dated 1947, and an affidavit that the applicant bought it from an American soldier in 1950. Pretty thin."

"So the folks trying to insure these paintings may not have an insurable interest?"

"With these many question marks, we would have to do a lot of work to establish authenticity. If we accept the applicant's valuations, which are based on the assumption that the paintings are authentic, and they are stolen or lost in a fire we will have to pay a lot of money and never know whether we were scammed or not. Even if the paintings are authentic, heirs of families and dealers that lost art during the war, have been pressing claims for restitution. The Russian decrees relating to art brought back to the USSR by the Red Army are not recognized in the West, so most paintings that disappeared during the War, and come out of Russia, carry with them built in issues of ownership. At the very least I would like to get legal involved before we go any further. Meanwhile, I will have one of our folks do a further investigation of these paintings so we can have a more complete picture of what we are dealing with."

"Okay, Kate, go ahead. Another good piece of work. Over lunch, no less. To think that majoring in art history at Harvard and all your gallery snooping and the lectures you attend would be so helpful to us here at L & M. And it wasn't even a factor in hiring you."

"Maybe I should apply to L & M for retroactive tuition reimbursement for the cost of sending me through Harvard."

"Lots of luck trying that. But there is something else I want to talk to you about. As you know the Paris office is a mess. They can't seem to close an investigation or get a report out to our partners. We had an Executive Committee meeting yesterday. We would like to ask you to go over there for a while and straighten it out."

"Paris, huh?"

"It could be good career move for you."

"While I indulge my first love? Art?"

"And your new love." Nick smiled. "I really like the guy."

Chapter Eight

"Nice shot, Sofia," said one of the two men kneeling beside her on a well-worn firing bench at the front of an old KGB shooting range outside of Moscow. "You outshot us with the Suchka, but I think Mikhail and I can beat you with the RPK-74, fired from the Spetsnaz position. After all, we were Spetsnaz. Let's see what you can do with the farthest targets up the hill."

Moving to the side of the bench, Sofia Mostov began in the kneeling position and then got on her side, extending one leg and holding the weapon parallel with the ground. She fired two shots from each position, followed by the two former soldiers.

Boris watched Sofia lithely move through each firing position. He also observed the congratulatory gestures from her two companions as they returned from the targets.

"Well, Boris," said one of the shooters, a beefy fifty-year old with a bald head and a two-day growth of beard, "she is as good a shot as you said she was. We could have used her in Afghanistan. We always thought you KGB types just used knives, poison and pistols!"

Boris Voroshilov smiled. "Perhaps you'd like to shoot for Vodka?"

The shooter held up his hands in mock horror. "My pension is small enough as it is!"

As Boris and Sofia climbed into his old Lada, he said, "Well *plemyanitsa* you haven't lost your touch, and you may need it. Your friend, Perez, wants to meet us in Paris next week to discuss our new art business. He and his colleagues are dangerous *hombres.*"

They drove through Moscow's chaotic traffic. Boris swerved across two lanes to avoid a car whose driver had decided to dodge a big Kamaz dump truck, and then honked at an old Mercedes whose driver had decided to circumvent a traffic jam by proceeding in the wrong lane against traffic. They soon discovered the tie-up was caused by police stopping traffic so a number of government cars, and some privately-owned Mercedes and BMW's, could drive unimpeded down the center lane.

As they walked into Boris's apartment in the Zamoskvorechye neighborhood of Moscow, Sofia commented, "Uncle, your decorating style never changes. This place reminds me of your Paris apartment near the Gare du Nord. Same overstuffed furniture. Same musty smell." She parted the curtains. "I am going to open some windows."

"*Plemyanitsa*, you always try to improve me."

"Yet you do not change."

"No, but Moscow does. And not for the better. I was sitting in a crowded tea room yesterday. Two women—they seemed young to me, but they were very attractive and so thin—were sitting at the next table. They wore lots of jewelry and had expensive mink coats draped over their shoulders. One of them said to the other something like, 'I love your purse. Is it new?' The other one said, 'Yes, he wants me to carry a Louis Vuitton bag all the time. He bought me three. I guess it makes him feel like he has big ones. I couldn't care less. They don't even have pockets inside for my stuff.' Then they got up and threw money on the table. Didn't even look at the bill. They got into a Bentley. Their driver probably drove in the center lane. I remember when that lane was only used by high government officials. Now you can buy access to it just like you can buy everything else in Moscow."

"Uncle, you are quite an eavesdropper."

"Old habits don't go away. Besides the tables are quite close together in that place."

Boris stood up and looked out the window of his apartment. Opening up a humidor, he selected a cigar, lit it, and then sat quietly for a few minutes. Taking a deep draft of the cigar, he said, "Sometimes I miss Cuba. If we were there instead of this continual traffic noise of today's Moscow, there would be music coming through our windows. I remember when I first brought you to this place many years ago."

"That park I played in as a girl is now gone."

"Replaced by a concrete monstrosity!" Boris shook his head. "I will get us some vodka to toast yesterday and our new venture."

As he poured vodka into small glasses, Sofia studied him. He wore the same outfit as always: dark pants, white shirt, and a sweater with a shawl collar. Five-foot seven, in his early seventies, with a gray beard and overweight but strongly built, he moved gracefully as he handed Sofia a glass of vodka and lowered himself into a large, well-worn reading chair.

"Uncle, you have only talked in broad outlines about this art deal you and Perez are discussing. Tell me more."

Boris let out a cloud of smoke and settled in his chair. "I will start by telling you how I first heard about it. You were still in Cuba after your escape from St. Barth. I was visited by someone I had worked with in our organization. This fellow was quite sick."

Boris took another deep draw on his cigar. Sofia focused on the long grey ash and wondered when it would fall off on her uncle's sweater, which bore evidence of other dropped ashes.

Evening was starting to fall outside the old apartment and the steady sound of Moscow traffic came through opened windows. Boris resumed his story. "He told me that he had an older brother who he wanted me to meet. A few days later he brought Andrei Androyov here. Shortly after my first meeting with Andre, too much vodka and too many cigarettes caught up with his brother. I went to his graveside funeral. The only mourners were three or four old operatives from the organization and his brother. No one else. At least his grave is marked. Such is the recognition one gets in today's Russia for many years of service.

"Over several more meetings, Andrei told me an amazing story that he said he had told no one except his brother. At the end of the war, he was part of a Red Army patrol that ambushed a small German convoy, east of Dresden. The convoy consisted of three empty trucks and two staff cars. They killed two German officers in the ambush and questioned the remaining soldiers. One of the soldiers said that they were returning to German lines after storing a large number of paintings in a cave. The German said that he knew where the cave was and even had a map. Andrei, his captain, and another young lieutenant, Nikolai, had the German take them to the cave. Andrei, who had worked at the Moscow museum before the war and knew something about art, was overwhelmed by what they found. A treasure trove of works the Nazis had stolen. He remembered a Matisse, a Monet, seventeenth century Dutch artists, a Picasso and many others."

"The Nazis must have been planning to come back after the war and retrieve the art," Sofia observed.

"Well, the captain sensed that they had stumbled on something of great value. He kept the map and shot the German. The three of them agreed to keep their find a secret. When they got back to their camp, they searched the Nazi colonel's body and found a list of the works. The captain whispered 'dead men keep secrets' to Andrei and ordered the remaining German soldiers shot. On the way back to their lines, they were attacked by German planes and the captain was killed.

Nikolai took the list and map off the captain and gave it to Andrei."

"What did he do with it?"

"Andrei sat on this find for a long time. His brother was stationed in Dresden before the wall went down, he eventually told him about the cave and they went back to try and find it. They succeeded. The art was untouched."

"And then?"

"The two brothers didn't know what to do and the younger brother was dying so he introduced Andrei to me. I went to Germany with Andrei to confirm the value of what they had found, and then quickly enlisted a few of our colleagues who appreciate a lucrative business opportunity in the effort to remove the paintings and truck them back to Moscow. We remodeled my old dacha into a secure storehouse and began the project. I will take you to the dacha tomorrow so you can see for yourself what we have."

"But why Perez?"

"A good question. As I worked on a plan for taking advantage of this incredible find, I determined that we needed to bring in a partner who could help us in some important ways. Because he participated with us in the jewelry business, I thought of Perez. He is knowledgeable about the art world, greedy and obsessed with laundering his drug money on a large scale. So, he can be useful to us. He has connections that will facilitate the sale of some of our merchandise in a confidential manner and he has an organization that can hide large transactions from unwelcome eyes. He also wants to open an art gallery in Italy that can be an important piece of the plan—and he has the capacity to finance some of the operation."

Sofia sat silently while Boris puffed on his cigar.

Chapter Nine

"Let's stop for some tea before we get to your dacha," Sofia instructed. "I want to go through our plans again."

"Okay, *plemyanitsa*, you are methodical as always."

Boris poured black tea into two glasses from a pot the waiter had filled from a large samovar in the corner of the small restaurant just off the highway. After squeezing a lemon slice into his tea, Boris took a bite out of a pastry. "Not up to Yeliseev's pastry, but not bad for a country restaurant."

"Uncle, I feel more secure talking here than in a big place like Yeliseev's. The area around Tverskaya Square is crowded—I am always looking over my shoulder."

"You are right, there are so many people now on the Moscow streets shopping that it is hard to know if anyone is following you. At least when the streets were uncrowded, one could do a competent job of surveillance." Sofia looked up at the frequently patched ceiling of the restaurant and then gazed at Boris. "Let's get back to how we deal with Perez. Can we trust him?"

"Sofia, whether or not I trust someone like Perez depends on how much he needs us. Over time he will see that we can be very valuable to him and as we say in Russia, 'if the hole is deep and it rains, the climb out is very slippery.' Tell me about your meeting with him in Mexico."

"He called me in Cuba after I left St. Barth in the

hurricane. I bantered with him a bit over the phone. He said that he called my jewelry store in St. Barth but all he got was a message in French that the store was temporarily closed. He groused that the message was not in Spanish. I asked if he had really called me in Cuba to complain about my store's answering machine. He laughed."

"A good thing—he doesn't laugh much."

"No, but even a hint of lightness in a man is good. It means he is open to a bit of flirtation. He is interested in me as a woman. The more interested in me he is, the more his judgment will be compromised."

"Ah, yes. Polovaya zapadnya. The honey trap. That was your first operation as I remember. In Angola, you lured that South African intelligence operative to your hotel room. Took off most of his clothes. We were in the next room behind a two-way mirror. We came in, showed him the film, and he gave us—and the Cubans—a lot of good information. Ah, the wiles of a woman."

"No, the weapons of a woman, Uncle, and it is just a weapon."

Boris smiled. "So, he invited you to meet with him in Mexico City."

"Roberto and I flew there in the Pilatus. He lives in a large, well-guarded house outside of the city. He has a lot of art and seemed quite knowledgeable as he took us through and talked about his collection. Some excellent works. He has a Diego Rivera, several pieces by Rivera's son-in-law, Rafael Coronel. He has a mural on a wall in his house by a famous Mexican muralist. He has contributed works to the museum in Mexico City and to a Mexican art museum in Chicago. He has two Picasso's that I saw, as well as a Monet, a Rothko and a number of other high-quality works. He has—how do the Americans say it—a chip on his shoulder about the way he was treated in business school in the United States."

"What do you mean—a chip on his shoulder?"

"He feels that he was under-valued because he was Mexican. And then, years later, the school stopped communicating with him after he was mentioned in some newspaper article about Mexican drug cartels."

"Interesting."

"Yes, it is something about him we can use."

"Ah, *plemyanitsa*, you remember your training. Study everyone. Identify vulnerabilities and use them. In his case, a taste for a beautiful woman like you, and whatever sense of inferiority he is hiding under his bluster may be helpful to us."

Sofia nodded, and then went on, "We talked about the problems the French police and that American insurance investigator, Catherine York, were giving us in the jewelry business. He described his role as primarily investing money from the profits of the white powder business, but that he had to clean a lot of money in the process. Finally, he complemented us on how the jewelry business was a way to clean money, and he wanted us to, in his words, as I remember them, 'come up with new approaches.' He said he would like to work with me as a partner. That he needed some new challenges. He joked that maybe the Stanford Business School would put him back on its mailing list. When we left, he gave me a very close and very long hug."

Voroshilov smiled and then said, "In London he took me to a very good meal at the Connaught Grill—he was staying at the hotel—and repeated that he wanted to partner with us. He asked about you and if you had any relationships."

"What did you tell him?"

"That you only have business relationships."

"That's all?"

"Well, you told him the truth."

"Like you, I sometimes tell the truth. Perez, as I said, can be a valuable part of our enterprise. We just have to be wary. He understands art. He is connected to the big spender international art scene and is now partnering with one of the Italian families to distribute heroin and cocaine in Italy. He didn't talk much about that and I don't want to know, but he thinks that there is big money to be made. And, given our problems with the French police, Italy is the best place in Europe for us to move art. And it is right across the Adriatic from Montenegro."

"You mentioned Montenegro a couple of weeks ago, but how does it fit into our plan?"

"We have to move art from Moscow into Europe and the best entry point is through Italy. But it would be dangerous to try to ship a large number of paintings directly into Italy through conventional means. Venice is becoming an international art center. And Montenegro can be a one-day boat trip from Venice, as well as from other ports on Italy's east coast. And most importantly our colleagues have excellent relations with the Montenegro government. It can be a secure base of operation. We just have to figure out the logistics of avoiding the Italian customs authorities." Boris stopped to pour more tea. "And there is another benefit that Perez brings—money. I don't want to rely too heavily on our Russian colleagues or use too much of our funds. We need to spread the risk a bit."

Sofia reached over and wiped some meringue from his beard. "It all makes sense. I agree that we have to watch Perez closely."

Boris smiled, put his hand over hers, "That is your task— keep close to him."

Sofia nodded and thought to herself, *but not too close.*

They got up from the table and resumed their trip west out of Moscow.

As they drove, Sofia said, "So Andrei and the other old soldier, this Nikolai, have quite different views about what to do with the paintings?"

"Very different. Andrei has a great interest in art and has probably thought often about the paintings that he and

Nikolai found in Germany at the end of the war. Andrei went to Germany with our trucks, guided them to the cave where the paintings were hidden and accompanied them on the trip back to Moscow. As our plan developed, Andrei brought his nephew, Sergei, into our little group. He raised Sergei as a son after his parents died when he was a young boy. He has tutored Sergei well. We needed a highly skilled artist and one we could trust. Sergei is both. You will meet him shortly."

Sofia studied Boris for a moment. *He never changes,* she thought; *he still looks like a little bear, his KGB name.* He seemed to her to have gained new energy from a new venture.

"Nikolai was uninterested in our plan at first, but is now vehemently opposed. I think he is losing it mentally. He called me to rant again the day before yesterday. I cut him off, but later met him for a drink in a bar near Arbat where he lives. He knows what we are going to do with the art, but in true Russian fashion he has obviously been brooding about it. Again—in the Russian way—the brooding has been followed by outbursts. He is convinced that we don't have the right to profit from the art. That the paintings belong to "The People"—his word. He has become a patriot and wants the art given to the state. After giving them no attention for years, he is now obsessed with the paintings. Nikolai could not only end our enterprise, but could get us all into a lot of trouble. He is a very stubborn old man—an idealist—and a stubborn idealist is a very dangerous person. We must address this problem before we meet with Perez in Paris."

"Has he talked to anyone else?"

"I just found out that he has consulted a lawyer of a particularly shady type named Alex Petrov. We will discuss the lawyer later, but it is not a good thing that Nikolai went to see him."

"What do you think we should do?"

"Nikolai is too great a risk. With his instability he could bring the whole thing down around us. We probably have to deal with him today. The remoteness of my dacha provides an opportunity."

"And Andrei?"

"Andrei is in full agreement with us and I would like to see him get some benefits from our efforts before he dies."

Boris drove the Lada through a wooded area and continued until the countryside grew hillier. Turning off the main road, he followed an unmarked side road and turned into a narrow gravel-covered driveway that led to a wooden structure partly obscured by dense stands of evergreens. A Volkswagen SUV, a battered Volga and a Peugeot were parked on one side.

Boris turned to Sofia. "Well, here we are. Brace yourself both for Nikolai and for the beauty of this collection. The Nazis were bastards, but they had good taste in what they stole."

Chapter Ten

OUTSIDE MOSCOW

Boris and Sofia walked onto a covered porch and then inside into a long narrow room furnished with rustic chairs, a few couches and several tables. The wood in the furniture was dark brown, matching the log walls, and the cushions on the chairs and couch were red and green leather. The long wall opposite the front door appeared to Sofia to be newly plastered. Tall bookcases stood against it. A few icons were placed on the spaces between the bookcases.

Boris led her around one corner to a large kitchen where three men sat silently at a round wooden table. A half-empty vodka bottle and three glasses were on the table. The room was silent. Two of the men were quite elderly. One, thin and bald with deep-set, almost black eyes, sat pushed away from the table, his arms tightly folded over his chest, glaring at the other two men.

"Sofia, these are our colleagues. This is Andrei," said Boris pointing to a grey-bearded overweight man who rose from the table. "And this is Nikolai," motioning to the slight man with the folded arms, who acknowledged her only with a grunt.

Sofia nodded to the two men and then to a third sitting to the side.

Boris continued. "And this is Sergei." The young man stood only after being prodded by his uncle. He was thin with a narrow face and dark beard that set off his very pale complexion. Sofia thought to herself that his skin looked almost translucent.

"Nikolai, it appears that you are still unhappy with our plan," said Boris.

"Your so-called plan is wrong, wrong!" said Nikolai, his face reddening as he talked. He pounded the table so hard the glasses and bottle shook and vodka spilled over the top of his glass onto the table. "You are taking what is not yours. It is the property of the Russian people."

"Nikolai, we have been over this many times before. I want to show Sofia the storeroom and then we can talk some more. Wait here for us. Sergei, come with us, but leave your glass on the table. We don't want any spills on the merchandise."

Boris, then led Sofia and Sergei around the corner from the kitchen into the hallway lined with bookcases. Removing several books from one of the bookcases, Boris pushed aside a part of the wall revealing an electronic panel. "Not very original, I know, but effective," said Boris with a shrug. He entered numbers on a keypad and then placed his hand over a grey pad at the bottom of the panel. Two bookcases parted revealing a steel door built flush into the wall. Boris opened the steel door. Reaching in, he turned on a light in a large room, motioned for Sofia and Sergei to follow him and closed the door behind them.

As Sofia's eyes adjusted to the fluorescent lighting, she saw that the room was long and narrow with steel racks covering the entire back wall facing the door. The rest of the room was filled with a large square work table.

"I apologize for the stuffy air, but we built this room to protect the art from damage by temperature or humidity changes or by excessive light, as well as to keep it secure. No one visiting would know what is hidden here in the center of this dacha."

"Uncle, how did you get them here from Germany?"

"We used trucks with the paintings secured behind crates

of mechanical equipment. Actually, some German-engineered components on the trucks were used to create the climate controls and elements of the ventilation system in this room. Not only did we benefit from fine German engineering, but there is no record here in Russia of our purchases."

"No problems with inspections on the trip to Moscow?"

"Of course not, our former associates saw to the logistics and helped with—shall I say—the remodeling of the dacha."

"Old friends helping old friends," said Sofia.

"Well, old friends who expect to profit handsomely from our enterprise."

"Ah, yes. Russia—some things never change."

"*Plemyanitsa*," said Boris, "you may be wondering why Sergei is here."

"He wouldn't be here unless you had a reason."

"Very true, very true," Boris laughed. "Sergei is a highly-trained and very-talented artist as well as possessing one of the keenest eyes in Russia for art that is authentic and that which is not. You are very knowledgeable about art, but this collection will impress you. Now let Sergei show you some of the merchandise. He has carefully catalogued and photographed each painting—and even done some research on estimated values."

For the next forty-five minutes, Sergei removed paintings from the racks and then placed them on easels that were lined up along the walls at each end of the room. Each painting had a note attached listing the artist and the date of the piece. Sergei commented on each painting as he placed it on the easel.

Pausing at one painting, Sofia said, "Isn't this a Matisse?"

"Yes it is," responded Sergei. "I saw some Matisses in Paris a few months ago. He was remarkable. This painting is from 1939. By then he had painted for a long time, yet this work would sell for a large sum."

"So, you follow the art market?" Sofia thought, *his eyes are so dark and his skin so white that he shows no emotion. He seems to know much about these paintings. He is hard to read.*

"I love to paint and to look at art. I leave the business end to Boris."

"Sergei doesn't care about money," said Boris. "He just cares about art, right Sergei?"

"Of course."

"This is an amazing collection," said Sofia, "and I have only seen part of it. In addition to the French, Spanish, Italian and Dutch artists, there are some excellent Russian artists represented. I recognize Larionov, Serov, Kandinsky and several canvasses by Ilia Dilinov. I'm surprised that there are paintings by Dilinov. As I remember he was in Paris only a short time before he came back to Moscow to join the army and was killed at the Front."

"That is correct, *plemyanitsa*, you are indeed a quick study. But Dilinov painted more pictures in both Paris and in Russia than is generally known, as well as some work he did while in the army." Boris winked at Sergei and said, "Please go back to the kitchen and try to keep your uncle and Nikolai from coming to blows. Few things are more absurd than two frail old men trying to hurt each other. Sofia and I have some matters to discuss. We will join you shortly."

After the door closed behind Sergei, Sofia said, "He seems to be very knowledgeable."

"He is quiet. He doesn't talk much. I don't think he has an interest in money. He cares about his uncle but his life is making pictures. He is a very skilled painter, and that is what is important to our enterprise. But we can talk about that later. Right now we need to think about Nikolai."

"So, you want me to deal with him?"

"Yes. Today. I don't want to risk waiting any longer. He is becoming a serious threat. Here is my plan."

They talked briefly and then reentered the kitchen. Andrei and Nikolai were shouting at each other. Nikolai was arguing that art seized by the Russian army belonged to the Russian state and that the military decrees at the end of the war declaring that all looted art seized by the Red Army belonged to the Soviet Union as war reparations and the legislation later passed by the Duma to the same effect was to be followed. Andrei disputed this, saying that the decrees and laws only related to claims of the original owners and that they, as the Russian *liberators* of the art could do as they pleased with it. Boris listened and watched, but made no effort to intervene even as Nikolai referred to him and Andrei as *criminals and looters.*

Nikolai pounded the table again and shouted, "I cannot let this second thievery happen." His face turning an ever-deepening shade of red, he got up from the table, knocked his chair over in the process and stormed out the door of the dacha. Boris motioned to Sofia to follow him, but she was already on her feet heading to the door.

Outside the dacha, Nikolai was walking to the battered old Volga. Sofia, her long legs rapidly closing the distance between her and Nikolai, while putting on a pair of gloves, called out, "Stop! I want to talk with you!"

Nikolai did not turn to face her but called over his shoulder as he reached his car, "I have nothing to say to you."

Or to anyone else, ever, thought Sofia. She grabbed him from behind and wrapped her left arm around his chest and jammed her left knee into the small of his back. She snapped his neck back until she heard the crack. Opening the passenger door of Nikolai's Volga, she picked up his body and put it in the passenger seat. She climbed in and started the car.

Several miles down a rutted dirt road, she pulled the car to a stop at the edge of a cliff overlooking a tree-filled ravine. She moved Nikolai's body into the driver's seat of the Volga and pushed the still running car over the edge of the cliff, watching as the old car tumbled down the steep embankment, turned upside down, skidded a short way on its roof and came to rest next to two large trees.

Shortly, Boris arrived. Looking down the cliff, he said "Goodbye Nikolai."

Climbing in the old Lada, Sofia said, "He was getting too old to drive safely anyway."

Boris thought to himself, *how green and beautiful were her eyes—and how cold. I was right to recruit her. She is the ideal operative—an orphan, tough and without emotion.*

Chapter Eleven

VENICE

Ettore Grassi, wearing an elegant hand-tailored tan suit, pale pink shirt and a patterned tie, approached the old man sitting on a bench at the tip of the Venetian island of Giudecca. Chin in hand, his thick white hair sticking out under his straw hat, the man was gazing across the narrow Canale della Grazia and toward the island of San Giorgio Maggiore. As Ettore approached, the old man stood to embrace him.

"*Ciao*, son."

"Padre, I always know to find you here, on your bench in the Campo Nani e Barbaro watching the ships. And always wearing that straw hat."

"Except in the winter when I wear a beret."

"Ah, yes, the beret."

"It keeps my head warm. The French think they invented the beret, but did you know it actually originated in the north of our country?"

"Well, Padre, they do take many of our good things—cuisine, painting and architecture—as their own."

"They also took a Veronese painting from the monastery there," he said, pointing to the island. "It is still in the Louvre. Maybe someday they will have the class to return it."

"Perhaps, Padre."

"They still don't understand how to live—*la bella vita*," he said, then sighed. "Come, sit with me and look out over Venice."

The two men sat close together. His father continued.

"I have lived in Venice all my life. But I always come back to this place. The tourists don't come here. Even to the church that Palladio designed. They look at it from San Marco but only a few bother to come to the island and go inside. So the Tintorettos are for us to savor. You know as I have told you many times, there are two Venices—the beautiful but sadly-fading city the visitors see and the inner Venice of all of us. We live in our city. They visit the other city. This island is part of our Venice like the neighborhood in Dorsoduro where you grew up."

"*Si*, you still live in that yellow house where I was born and where Madre, bless her memory, died."

"Of course. Where else would I live? And I still have a boat so I can cruise the lagoon and look at the islands—once so much a part of Venice and now so many of them deserted except for the rats and the derelicts. But enough of the memories and sadness of an old man. Talk to me about the Mexicans. How goes it with this Francesco Perez? I hear that our arrangement to distribute their product in the north is working well—so well that it is getting the attention of the police."

"We are making a lot of money as you know. But, I don't think it will be stable for much longer. They are very aggressive and I am sure they are thinking that they could take over distribution in the whole country."

The old man snapped his fingers. "Poof—there goes our arrangement with the Southerners—they stay south, we stay north. It has given us some measure of peace, although we are starting to rub up against each other in Rome. But, I have another concern about the current situation. I have been around for a long time. You have done a fine job of taking over running our business, and it has given me time to sit on my bench, and observe things and think—*il dolce far niente*."

The old man stood up, stretched, took off his weathered straw hat and ran his fingers through his hair.

"This business is about surviving and prospering over the long run. During the war we worked with the Americans because we were convinced that they would defeat the Germans. So, we had access to many items that others could not get. We sold radios, tires, trucks, food and many other items at a profit. We looked ahead. In the same way we have worked over many years with the Italian governments. The governments come and go. We stay. I think it was a Sicilian writer who said for things to stay the same they must change."

"A very Italian observation."

"Ettore, look at that large cruise ship on the Fondamenta."

"What about it, Padre?"

"Thirty-forty years ago, most Europeans traveled by train. But some people foresaw the growth of travel by cruise ships because they realized that people were becoming wealthier—and older—like me, and they would want to vacation on cruise ships. Some built ships, others built piers to accommodate them. Now no one vacations by train— they take cruises or they fly on big planes paying little for their seats. In America I am told they are converting train stations to shopping malls. Travel continues but the way people travel will change."

Ettore, who was listening intently, said, "Padre, when was the last time you flew on an airplane?"

"Hah. I don't see how they can fly so I don't use them. But I am more than happy to make money from fuel, construction contracts, the food they serve their passengers, airport fees."

"Padre, where are you going with all this?"

"Ettore, the Mexicans are obsolete, like train travel vacations. Their business model won't work over time. Soon, we will not need them."

"Where will we get the merchandise?"

"From your cousin's laboratory."

Ettore Grassi cocked his head and looked at his father who was staring over the water at San Marco. The old man's brother had not gone into the family business. Having a scholarly bent, he had gone to graduate school and earned a doctorate in chemistry from the University of Bologna. Ettore's cousin followed his father into chemistry, but he also was drawn to the work of his uncle. He was now producing designer drugs in his laboratory in San Marino on Italy's east coast. The organization was starting to distribute this product in its territory, and Ettore thought to himself, *at very good profits.*

"Think of it, *figlio*. It is the future. No shipments of powder with all the risk. Instant pills! Whatever highs people want, we will be able to give it to them. In aspirin bottles! Low cost, low risk, high profits. By concentrating on this market, we won't need the Mexicans, and both our own forms of persuasion and simple economics will force them out—maybe with a little help from our friends in government."

"And their expansion will stop."

"*Essattamente.* And so will their violent ways. We cannot allow a plague to overtake us. A plague of unnecessary and brutal violence that will force the government to get involved. An undesirable outcome. And that is what the Mexicans—and for that matter—the Russians will bring us."

The two men were then silent. The sound of the water lapping against the cement Fondamenta and the engines of boats the only sounds. Then his father asked, "Ettore, where are you taking Perez to dinner?"

"He is falling in love with all things Italian, and he wants to try Venetian cuisine, so we will eat at a place on the San Basilio."

"I think I know the place—near Cala Chiesa, across from the church with the Veronese paintings. Wonderful sardines."

"*Si.*"

"On your way to the vaporetto, you might stop at the

Redentore Church and light a candle. After all, the church was built to thank the Lord for saving Venice from the plague."

Ettore hugged his father and walked along the Fondazione San Giovanni to the Zitelle vaporetto stop where he boarded a Number 8 for the short trip to the Redentore stop.

Chapter Twelve

Outside of Moscow

Sofia and Boris left a café in the Zamoskvoreche district of Moscow and began to walk. Boris said, "I like this neighborhood. It still has the feel of the Moscow I remember when I was young." His face darkened. "Petrov called me yesterday. The greedy bastard wants to get his cut. We have to deal with him."

"Knowing you Uncle, you have a plan."

"Well, *Plemyanitsa*, while you have been studying some of the works at the Tretyakov," he waved his hand toward the West, "I have been doing a bit of investigating. I had two objectives. First, to try to make sure that he hadn't talked to anyone else about the art and, second, to learn something about him that we could use in eliminating him."

"And?"

"I called on some of our former colleagues and we searched his offices and installed listening devices. As far as I can tell, he has kept his mouth shut. But we scored a bonus. He is active as a middleman in passing money to some of our hardworking Moscow officials. Nothing too big. But our colleagues are very pleased that they can add information to their dossiers on these officials, who will now become very cooperative. As to his habits, it turns out that he loves to take saunas, says he takes one a day. So I told him that I like saunas too, although of course I really despise them. It was easy to lead him to suggest that I join him. He suggested we meet at a small bath-house near his dacha, not too far from here."

"Is it safe?" Sofia said.

"I stopped by and looked at it. It is a good place to meet. Deserted in the evening. I will set up an appointment with him for tomorrow night."

Taking a map out of his pocket, Boris pointed out to Sofia the location of the bathhouse. "I am to meet him there at 7:00 tomorrow evening. You arrive there at 7:15, and here is what we will do."

Boris leaned his head close to hers and talked to her in a hushed tone.

"Now let us finish our walk. I will try not to look at the Starbucks on the corner. And in an old part of Moscow..." he said and shook his head.

◆ ◆ ◆

The bathhouse favored by the lawyer, Petrov, was about two miles off one of the highways headed north from Moscow. It was a small non-descript one-story building made of logs carelessly chinked with fading cement, some of the logs had been patched with slabs of non-matching wood hammered in place. The door was flanked by two dirty windows covered by equally dirty curtains. On each side there were several scrawny birch trees and a few pines. The bathhouse's neighbors were a run-down auto garage and a rusting metal storage building. When Boris arrived the only car in the parking area in front of the building was a late-model Mercedes that Boris surmised was owned by the lawyer. *He lives well but he could find a better bathhouse,* thought Boris.

Entering through the unlocked door into a small room, Boris saw a bottle of vodka and a tin of caviar in an ice bucket on a well-used desk where he guessed the attendant sat.

Boris went into the changing room where Petrov's clothes hung on a peg. Removing his clothes he wrapped himself in a towel and opened the heavy sauna door made of sturdy planks of rough wood. He could barely make Petrov out through the steam rising from the water-splashed hot coals. The steam and the sauna's wet wood produced a fragrance that Boris always associated with the forests of Russia after a summer rain.

"Hello Voroshilov," said Petrov. "Enjoy the steam, although the room has not yet heated up sufficiently."

"Oh, it will," said Boris.

"Did you see my treats out there?"

Boris nodded.

"When our pores are open and clean, we can drink some vodka, eat and talk about business and I would like to see the art that Nikolai has told me about. He says that it is not far from here."

"Of course. But you are certain that Nikolai has not discussed this with anyone else?"

"Absolutely, I cautioned him about secrecy at our first meeting and I have told no one. The fewer who know the more profit for us."

Boris thought he could see Petrov through the steam rubbing his hands together.

After a few minutes, Boris stood up, poured water on the coals and said, "We need another bucket of water. I will be right back." He wrapped his towel around him, pushed the wooden handle of the door open and exited the sauna. He walked to the front room, opened the door and waved in Sofia. They went down the corridor where Boris pointed out the heavy wooden beam that was used to secure the door when the sauna was not in use. The beam was held in place by two large metal brackets on each side of the sauna door frame. Motioning to Sofia, they lifted the beam and secured it in place. Sofia then turned the sauna heat regulator dial to its maximum setting of 60 degrees Celsius while Boris quickly dressed.

"Boris," came a voice from inside. "It is warm enough. Bring the vodka with you."

Boris picked up the bottle and looked at Sofia. "Good idea," he said as they walked out.

◆　◆　◆

Early the next morning, Boris and Sofia went back to the bathhouse. "The attendant is not yet here," said Boris. "He won't come to open the place up until this afternoon." They put on the gloves they had worn the previous evening, removed the heavy beam and turned the heat regulator down.

"Do you want to look inside?" asked Boris.

"No thanks," responded Sofia. "I like my lobster served in the shell."

Boris opened the door and looked in. He saw Petrov lying face down on the floor of the sauna—one leg caught on the lowest step. He closed the door and said to Sofia, "I don't know if he is a party member, but he's certainly a red lawyer."

They drove back to Boris's apartment, and after Boris secured the Lada, they entered the Novokuznetskaya metro station and took the subway to the Belorussky train station and their sleeper car to Paris.

Chapter Thirteen

Pierre Abou and Gerard de Rochenoir arrived at the small restaurant at the same time. The restaurant was on a short street off the Rue de Castiglione near the Place Vendome. It had a long bar on the right and several well-used tables along the left side and more tables in the small room beyond the bar. The two detectives embraced one of the proprietors who walked with them to a corner table.

"It has been too long Inspector de Rochenoir" said Marie, "and Pierre has only come in for lunch once in the past several weeks. Have you found a better place in Paris for steak au poivre?"

"There *is* no better place in Paris for steak au poivre, my dear Marie," said Gerard, bowing and kissing her hand as she beamed. "I have been in the United States for an extended visit and Detective Abou has had to solve all crimes in Paris singlehandedly, so he has had little time for lunch."

"No true Frenchman has too little time for lunch," boomed a voice from the back of the restaurant. Marie's barrel-chested, mustached husband came out wiping his hands on his dirty apron and put his big arms around the two detectives. "Welcome!" he bellowed.

Holding Michel at arms-length, Gerard said, "Okay, Michel, not too close. Pierre and I have to meet with an Italian cop in a few hours. I wouldn't want him to see me with

Parisian steak sauce on my shirt, even if your sauce is a national treasure."

"An Italian!" Michel snorted. "They come in here wearing pointy shoes and order veal picatta or something equally delicate. But I have some news for you. I would have passed this on to Pierre, but he hasn't shown up much over the past few weeks."

"He has been busy. What have you been hearing?"

"Some grumbling about Mexicans and drug stuff."

"Michel," shouted Marie, "the place is starting to fill up. No more gossip. And put on a clean apron."

Pierre laughed and said, "Michel we don't want to get into trouble with Marie. I will come by and drink some wine with you after you close this afternoon."

After they sat down, Gerard said, "Our distinguished visitor from Italy will be at the office in about two hours. It is not often that we get a request for a meeting from Italy's Minister of the Interior."

"No, it's unusual. According to what I was told, our visitor is a senior official in the Anti-Drug Central Directorate of the Italian State Police. His trip here is apparently connected to the murders in Marseilles that I have been working on."

"Any recent developments in that case?"

"No, although the ace investigators in the Marseilles force have now concluded that the killings were not part of a Marseilles gang dispute."

"Which was your conclusion from the beginning."

Pierre shrugged his shoulders.

Gerard sat silently, then said, "Pierre, you have some sauce on your tie. Here is a napkin." As Pierre rubbed his tie, spreading the stain over a wide area, Gerard watched in dismay. "Time to get back to work." He led the way to the front of the restaurant and handed Marie several Euro notes. "Tell Michel that his steak is wonderful as always and the wine you selected was superb!"

"Thank you Senior Inspector. You and Pierre should no longer be strangers. I just received some wine from Bordeaux that I think even you will find superb. And, Pierre, bring your wife. Senior Inspector, please come with one of those beautiful women whom I hear you occasionally take to dinner."

"Marie, it would be an honor. I have someone in mind."

The two exited and walked along the Rue de Rivoli crossing the Tuilleries in front of the Louvre on their way to the Île de la Cité and police headquarters.

◆　◆　◆

Assistant Director Steffani Terzazo of the Anti-Drug Central Directorate of the Italian Polizia de Stato followed an unsmiling woman past two security checkpoints and down several drab hallways, then up three floors past a reception desk to a tall unmarked door. It opened into a small room with a desk, file cabinets and a chair for visitors. She motioned him to wait, knocked on an inner door and a few minutes later a tall grey-haired man wearing a perfectly fitting black suit with a patterned white shirt and a rose-colored tie entered the room. "I am Senior Inspector Gerard de Rochenoir. Welcome to Paris. Please come into my office."

The first thing Terzazo noticed was the beautiful semi-circular walnut desk facing the door. The carpet was an old Persian in warm shades of gold, grey and deep red. On the wall were several abstract prints and a medieval map of Paris. The only indications that this elegant office, a severe contrast to the rest of the building, was that of a police officer, were the police publications in French and English neatly shelved in a wooden bookcase and a collection of handcuffs mounted on a display board and hanging in direct view of the chairs facing the desk.

Against a wall stood a stocky, broad-shouldered man, his arms folded over his chest, wearing a wrinkled brown suit and a tie with a prominent grease stain on it. Gerard introduced Terzazo to Pierre.

"You have a very pleasant office, Senior Inspector de Ro-chenoir. Your view of Notre Dame is spectacular and the handcuffs a nice touch."

"Thank you, Assistant Director. The handcuffs are a subtle reminder to some of the people who sit across the desk from me. The view of the Cathedral helps me to keep my perspective. No matter what evil our criminals perpetrate, it reminds me that man is also capable of a life of the spirit and of creating great beauty."

"A noble sentiment, one I will keep in mind in my work."

"But, Assistant Director, tell us what brings you here. We know little of the reason for your visit, other than that the request for the meeting came from a very senior official in the Italian government."

"There is a file I want to leave with you. It contains details of what I'm about to discuss." Terzazo leaned over to open the clasp on his brown leather brief case. Gerard observed his visitor.

Terzazo was of medium height with greying hair, cut short almost to a military length. His eyes were green, and subtle wrinkles were beginning to form at their corners. Gerard thought he was probably in his mid-forties. His blue suit, to Gerard's discerning eye, was hand-made as was his blue-and-white-striped shirt complemented by a tie of deep maroon. He wore highly polished black slip-ons with stockings that matched the color of his suit. His cufflinks were silver as was his Panerai watch. On his lapel was a small pin in the shape of a shield which Gerard observed was likely worn only by senior members of the Italian State Police. He appeared trim and moved with an athletic grace.

Terzazo handed each detective a card and thanked them for taking the time to meet with him. He also brought Gerard greetings from one of his colleagues with whom Gerard served on an Interpol task force. He placed a thin file folder marked "Confidenziale" on Gerard's desk and moved his chair back slightly so he could face both Gerard and the now seated Pierre.

Speaking excellent French, he began. "We have been observing for some time and with increasing concern the apparent growth of drug trafficking in the North of our country. We have come to believe that there are new players in the business who are working with some of the established dealers but who are also challenging a long-time player operating out of Naples in the Italian south. Recently, there has been an upsurge of violence in the south. Two members of the gang in the south were found murdered in Naples one week ago. The crimes were committed with a brutality—beheadings—that was clearly the work of people who were sending a message. The two men murdered in Marseilles last month—Detective Abou is familiar with the case—were both from the Camorra in Naples. What were they doing in France where they have never operated? We think that the increased volume of purer heroin we're starting to see may be entering Europe through Marseilles.

"One of our operatives believes the Mexican cartels are becoming involved in Italy. They are apparently the new players. We know that you have been keeping watch on these cartels here in France. We felt it would be prudent to work together and share intelligence. We certainly need your help if the contraband is coming in through Marseilles, and it would be helpful if we could find out what you have discovered about the Marseilles murders. We are prepared to share our information with you." He pointed to the file on Gerard's desk.

"Do you think the Naples and Marseilles murders are connected?" asked Gerard.

"If these two sets of murders are connected to drug dealing in Italy, and if there is drug smuggling in Marseilles that is reaching into Italy, I do think that we have a mutual interest."

"Assistant Director Terzazo, I would have to agree with you. The Marseilles murders cannot be explained by simple territory disputes in Marseilles. You come here highly recommended, and I am authorized to initiate a cooperation with you if I am satisfied that such an undertaking is prudent." Gerard paused and looked up at the plastered ceiling of his office before bringing his gaze directly on the Italian policeman. "I must feel confident that our communications can be kept confidential. I apologize for my frankness, but…"

Terzazo interrupted. "Senior Inspector Rochenoir, I understand, and I can assure you of the integrity of anyone on my team with whom you might interact. Containing the drug trade is the function of my department. We report directly to the Minister of the Interior."

"Thank you for understanding my somewhat indelicate comments. I appreciate your assurances. Pierre, please explain to the Assistant Director what we know and what we suspect regarding the Marseilles murders."

An hour later, after handshakes, Terzazo was escorted out of Gerard's office with an understanding that the two teams would meet again as developments warranted.

When the two French detectives were alone, Gerard stood up and looked out of his office window across the Rue d'Arcole at the façade of Notre Dame. "I never tire of this view, Pierre. Sometimes I think my life revolves around that church. My office faces it, I walk past it almost every day on my way to this building, my parents prayed there for many years. Notre Dame seems timeless and a refuge from the violent and sordid world you and I live in on a daily basis."

"If it wasn't for policemen like you and me, how much more violent and sordid would the world be? My parents are proud of me—although they have no real understanding of what I do. My father's life is my mother and his fishing boat." Now standing next to Gerard at the window, Pierre continued, "Those tourists milling around the Place du Parvis and the faithful waiting for Mass—they have a sense of security in their day-to-day lives without thinking for a moment of what it takes to give them that security."

"Pierre, the more we work together, the more I appreciate your perceptiveness. And now it appears that two murders in Marseilles will immerse us in the darkness of narcotics and the ambiguities of a criminal investigation in Italy. Never an easy place to work. I prefer the British police, even though some of them seem to think they invented criminal investigations. But, perhaps your friend, Mr. Holmes, will be of help to us."

Smiling, Pierre said, "You seem to be confident about working with this Italian cop."

"Terzazo is well thought of by their Minister of Interior, he seemed surprisingly candid, but we only saw his surface. Besides, what choice do we have?"

Chapter Fourteen

Venice

Ettore stood outside the marble façade of the Redentore, thinking how wise the architect, Palladio, was to locate it where the afternoon sun would glisten against the white marble. He then joined a group of Japanese tourists as they crowded on the vaporetto for the trip along the island and then across the canal to the Zattere stop, where he let the jostling crowd exit the vaporetto.

Grassi overheard a headwaiter engaged in a spirited discussion with an Italian who was directing a Japanese tour. The tour director was trying to get the headwaiter to look at his clipboard as he explained that they only had one hour for dinner before they were expected at the Peggy Guggeheim Museum. The headwaiter had his arms folded over his chest and was shaking his head vigorously. The tourists were oblivious to the discussion as they took pictures of each other with the Giudecca canal as the backdrop.

Grassi studied the expensive clothing in the windows of a shop on the San Trovaso canal, then crossed the bridge and looked over at the St. Trovaso Church, wondering whether the guide for the Japanese tour would take his charges past the church as they made their way to the museum. If they did, would they notice the two identical façades built so two rival families could each have their own entrance? He thought that such a hurried tour of Venice would miss the subtlety of the connection between the city's history and so much of its architecture.

He continued along the Fondamenta which widened at the Palazzo Molin where he turned to walk across a small campo. He then entered a restaurant on the second floor of a building that overlooked the San Sebastiano canal. Opposite the restaurant was the Church of San Sebastiano. He studied the church and the canal from a table on a small balcony that he had chosen both for the view and because of its privacy.

Another subtlety of Venice, he thought, *an unassuming façade of white stone facing a graceful bridge over the canal, and containing a number of wonderful paintings by his father's favorite artist, Veronese, who was buried in the church.*

He looked at the gondolas below him with their colorful carpets, fringed seats, black hulls and fanciful gold sea creatures on their bows. Jumbled together at the edge of the canal, their apparent disorder was comforting to Grassi because he knew that there was an organization to the massed gondolas that was apparent only to the true Venetian.

Lying across one of the gondolas, a gondolier was taking a nap. His bright red-striped shirt stood out against the black and dark blue of his gondola, his head on two pillows and his bare feet propped on the side of the boat, lulled to sleep perhaps by the gentle bobbing of his boat in the early evening breeze. A few feet away, another gondolier was sponging off his boat with water from an old pail.

Ettore's reverie was interrupted by Francesco Perez, who made his entrance wearing an open-collar shirt and a white sport jacket with large blue checks. Grassi thought to himself that Perez was one of those people who could not walk into a room quietly—or dress with subtlety.

"Ettore, you picked a hard place to find. I left the Gritti Palace, missed a turn over a canal and found myself looking at the La Fenice opera house. Then I went all the way to the Campo S. Angelo," he pointed to his map, "walked to a large square, and finally found the Accademia Bridge. I then walked all the way to that big canal and finally found the Molin Palace and this restaurant. I'm exhausted; this is a hard city to find your way around. I'm glad I allowed myself some extra time."

"Getting lost is the only way to get to know Venice. You will soon figure it out. Venice is two mazes, Francesco. First there are passageways—narrow, often leading to dead ends." Pointing to Perez's map he said, "By missing that small bridge over the San Maurizio Canal, you had to go all the way to the Campo S. Angelo before you could get back to the Accademia Bridge, which is one of only two over the Grand Canal until you get to the train station. The second maze is the canals where there are bridges that sometimes send you in the direction you want to go and sometimes don't." He looked at Francesco for recognition. "You look like you need a drink. I will order some wine."

"How about a Bellini? Last night I went to Harry's bar and had my first Bellini—and my second and third! I will bring that drink back to Mexico."

"If you had three, we'll have to raise the price of our merchandise. At Harry's, it's the most expensive cocktail in Venice."

"But this is Italy. You live well and sometimes the good life costs. But what is the secret of the drink?"

"The old man, Cipriani, invented the drink when, after the war, someone brought him some white peaches from France. He pressed them to get peach juice, mixed the juice with dry Prosecco —the best Prosecco comes from this region—and soon the cocktail became very popular. The more popular, the more expensive."

"Sort of like our product."

Grassi then signaled to a waiter standing just outside the door to the balcony and ordered the Bellinis.

"You came alone. No sturdy companion?"

Perez laughed. "I gave him the night off. I feel safe in Venice having dinner with you. After all, this is the city of your birth, and your father is a legend here and elsewhere in Italy. How is he?"

"He never changes," said Grassi, then thought to himself, *he just adapts.*

"Bless him. What do you recommend we have for dinner? And I congratulate you on your choice of tables. We are alone on this balcony."

"I like privacy. And this place is quiet. The tourists rarely come here."

Perez looked down at the gondolas in the canal. "Does anyone except tourists ever ride in gondolas?"

"Most visitors to Venice want to take a gondola ride but few realize the significance of the gondoliers. My father says that gondoliers represent the traditions of Venice more than anything else. I think he respects them because they do not change."

Perez stared at the gondoliers for a few minutes. "But it's such an inefficient way to get around. These motorboats are faster and more private. One can have a drink in a motorboat and put his arm around a beautiful woman on one of the couches. And how does a gondolier get access to a boat? Who does he pay? And why hasn't someone gotten control of the licenses and charged the gondoliers and their customers more for the pleasure?"

Grazzi thought to himself, *And to think that I even fleetingly considered bringing my father to this dinner. Perez would be swimming in the canal.*

After taking a long drink of wine, Grazzi moved the discussion to the status of their partnership.

Perez spoke enthusiastically of expanding distribution east into Slovenia and Croatia and also into southern Italy. As Grassi listened he thought to himself, *this man is very greedy and aggressive; every place he wants to go there are established operations.*

He wants more territory and that means war, which as his men demonstrated in Marseilles, he does not try to avoid. We are already pushing the southerners to the limit. Not good. I want to die peacefully in Milan or Venice—in my bed. As he was musing, the Bellinis arrived—a perfect peach color—in tall clear chilled flutes, the bubbles from the Prosecco streaming upward toward the rim. They toasted their enterprise and savored the Bellinis as the menus were placed discretely on the side of the table.

"Ettore, as you did so well in Milan, please order for us. I want to learn about the food and wine of this—today's eastern border of our empire."

Ah, yes, today's border, thought Grassi, then he responded to Perez, "It would be my privilege. Venice is the sea and the sea is Venice. Much of what we eat here is fish. So we will begin with fresh sardines. This restaurant is known for its steamed sardines—*al vapore,* as we say. They make a sauce out of lemon juice, garlic, capers, olive oil and parsley. After that, because it is in season now, some chilled white asparagus. And the wines of this area, which consists of three regions, are perhaps the best in Italy. We will have a white from the north of here called Friulano. The wine from this producer, which is unblended, you can only get in a few restaurants in Venice and perhaps Milan and Rome. Then another fish but one with a flavor much different from sardines. Monkfish is delicate and is prepared here very simply with a ginger vinaigrette and dill leaves. To pair with this dish, we will have a very full and flavorful Sauvignon Blanc."

Grassi motioned for the waiter and engaged him in rapid-fire Italian in the Venetian dialect that Perez could not follow. "Okay," Grassi said, "the chef just got some local duck, so I've also ordered duck breast for us. He likes to prepare it with pink peppercorns. Do you take your duck on the rare side?"

"*Si,*" said Perez.

"Good, because he sautés it on each side for just a short time."

"What wine do you recommend?"

"We will be drinking great white wines, but this area produces excellent red wines as well. I will order a Schioppettino, a concentrated red that may work well with duck.

"Finally, they serve very good Venetian pastries here. We can enjoy them with a local sweet wine such as a Valpolicella, the recioto style, or a less well-known but superb dessert wine made close by, called Torcolato."

Silent while Grassi ordered, Perez said, "With this wonderful food and the business opportunities here in Venice, just waiting to be exploited, I may never leave."

Perez looked over the balcony to the canal, "In fact, I am considering opening an art gallery in Venice."

"Francesco, the cuisine of Venice is wonderful, but an art gallery here is entirely a different matter. I saw many paintings in your villa in Mexico City. You are obviously a sophisticated collector. But I didn't know that you were interested in the business of art. Perez, I know you—what is the money angle?"

"The sale of art is an excellent way to move money. We are constantly looking for ways to accomplish that goal. We recently got into the thoroughbred horse business in the United States. Paintings, horses; the economics are the same. People buy because of the names of the artists and the bloodlines of the horses."

Grassi said, "Ah, very smart. The dirty money is mixed in with the profits from the business, and comes out clean. It is like selling appliances. But how do you achieve that with art?"

"Each piece is expensive and many transactions are conducted in secret with anonymous sellers and buyers. The seller is a private collector, as is the buyer. The painting is easily moved across borders. Hell, you just roll it up and put it in a tube. The transaction is never reported.

"A gallery can be very useful. I buy a painting with money I want to clean. Or I buy a building to house my gallery and a warehouse which I rent out and later resell. The money is laundered. No reporting and in Italy we don't pay much attention to the tax laws. And I have access to much art inventory so I can do business in volume."

Perez stopped talking long enough to take a bite of the sardines and exclaimed, "These are wonderful. Most sardines I have eaten come from cans. Do other restaurants here serve them?"

"Of course. There is a place near the Campo San Barbara that serves sardines in several marinades. It is a short walk from your hotel. And the chef's seafood is excellent as is the wine list."

Grassi looked at the canal again and took a sip of a wine the color of light gold. Then, with an effort to control his voice he said, "I can understand you wanting to open a gallery in Italy—but why Venice?"

Perez smiled and said, "Ettore, if I didn't know better, I might think that you don't want me to do business in this city. I have come to appreciate Venice. And the location—location is everything—right on the Adriatic, close to Trieste on the north, Montenegro toward the south. It will appeal to my Russian partners. I also thought of Paris and had scouted out a location on the Avenue Matignon. You know the street?"

"I think so, near the **Élysée** Palace. Many galleries. Seems like an excellent location."

"It is, but the French police have not been very welcoming to me. They even searched my house in Paris. Maybe they don't like Mexicans. So I have a French partner in Paris for the art business we do there."

Interessante, thought Grassi. He smiled at Perez. "Let's try the monkfish and discuss the current status of our partnership."

The two men ate and talked as the soft Venetian evening closed in around them.

Chapter Fifteen

PARIS

Mark Libidoux shifted his considerable bulk trying to find a comfortable perch on a small chair in a patisserie just off the rue St. Honore close to the rue Royale.

"Monsieur Libidoux, you look uncomfortable," said a waitress in a black skirt and blouse and a white apron.

"Yvonne, I have been coming here for years and I can never get used to these small chairs and wicker bottoms that feel like they are going to collapse at any minute. This place needs new chairs."

Smiling, the waitress replied, "I have been employed here for over thirty years, and the chairs have never been changed. I could probably work here for another thirty years and they still won't be changed."

"Ah *oui*, but the wonderful macarons don't change either, and it is worth a bit of discomfort to enjoy them. Each cookie is so crunchy on the outside and soft on the inside. And the filling between the two cookies—that wonderful ganache! Which flavors are you featuring this morning?"

"Today, we have grand marnier, raspberry, and coconut and white chocolate. Of course, we always have almond, lemon cream, and chocolate."

"Oh my. I can't decide ... oh please serve me one of each of your featured flavors and a lemon crème as well. And of course, a coffee."

Finishing his five macaroons, Marc Libidoux left the patisserie and turned onto the rue St. Honore, walked past the L'Elysee palace and entered a door just before he reached the Avenue Matignon. Taking the elevator to the second floor, he entered the Gallerie Libidoux. Waiting for him in a small reception area was a tall, blonde woman he had never seen before and Boris Voroshilov. Standing up, Voroshilov said in French with a heavy Russian accent, "Bon jour, Marc. Let me introduce you to Sofia Mostov."

"Ah, Madame Mostov, I have heard much about you from your uncle. I am charmed to meet you. I am sorry to be late, but…I had another engagement. Please come into my office. Ah, here is Perez."

As the four sat down at Libidoux's conference table, he began. "Boris, I have studied the inventory of the work you have in detail. The art you have is exceptional, but selling it will not be easy. There is a lot of sensitivity about works that the Nazis stole. All those lawsuits in New York and Vienna over the Gustav Klimts are examples of what can happen if a relative of a poor devil whom the Nazis killed shows up and claims a work as belonging to his family."

"Publicity isn't all bad," interjected Perez. "The restitution claim, the compensation payment the Austrian government complained was way too high, the transactions involving the Bloch Bauer heirs all resulted as I remember in Christie's selling five Klimts—each well above the presale estimate."

"We have to be cautious," said Boris. "There is an old Russian saying that when the owl screeches, the hunter pisses on his boot. For us, publicity would be a big problem if it caught the attention of certain people in Russia."

"I thought you had taken care of that problem," said Libidoux.

"We have with the people we think need to be brought into the deal," replied Boris, "but in today's Russia there are many vultures circling in the sky."

Looking at Boris and Sofia, Libidoux said, "What is the risk that some group in Moscow might seize the inventory?"

Sofia turned to Perez. "Francesco, in Moscow we discussed that risk. The plan that Boris has been working on involves your proposed gallery in Venice. Have you made any progress on that end?" Sofia, having taken off her jacket, was wearing a low-cut blouse from the French designer, Anne Fontaine, that had caught Perez's attention. Boris watched Perez's attention shift from her cleavage to her question.

"Yes, I have scouted some locations. I am interested in the Castello area near the canal. Perhaps with a view of San Giorgio Maggiore."

"Don't find a spot too close to the Questura," interjected Boris.

"The closer to the police headquarters, the safer we will be from thieves."

The group laughed at Sofia's comment and she continued to say that she liked a location that was convenient to the site of the Venice Biennale that would soon be in full force.

Libidoux looked anxious. "I will show some of your pieces here, but I would like for us to find a dealer in New York or London. Venice is not seen as a center for expensive modern art."

"Marc," said Perez, "bringing another dealer into our circle would increase the risk greatly. Venice is changing and the art scene there is quite lively. During the Biennale is a perfect time to open a gallery. We could be pioneers of big-time art in Venice and get the first mover advantage."

"Or the arrows," Libidoux mumbled and then said, "So, Francesco, how is your *other* business going in Italy?"

Perez didn't immediately answer, rather he stared at Libidoux. Sofia, always the keen observer, thought to herself that Francesco Perez was one of the few people she had met whose eyes actually changed color reflecting his emotional state. Perez lowered his gaze toward Libidoux, his normally grey eyes turning black as he replied in a tone that he was obviously forcing to keep level, "Libidoux, my business in Italy is completely separate from the enterprise we are meeting about. You are not to ask questions or to discuss me or my business with anyone outside of this room. To do otherwise would not be a good thing for me or for you." Then, switching from English to French, after a pause, *"Comprenez-vous?"*

Libidoux raised two fleshy hands off the table in a gesture Sofia understood to be submission and nodded his head. Then, continuing in French, *"Excusez-moi. Je suis désolée de vous avoir dérangé."*

"I was not disturbed, but I thought it prudent to warn you of the dangerous area you were approaching. Let's look at some more photos from Boris and then you can take us to lunch."

"Yes, I have arranged for a private room at a small place near here on the Rue de Berri. I will give you directions since we should probably arrive separately."

A bit later, sitting in the back room of a restaurant not far from the Avenue Matignon, the conversation turned to French interest in Russian art.

Boris responded to a question from Perez who had said little except to order a large plate of gnocchi with white truffles, "Francesco, the French have always had a special interest in Russia and Russian art. Why, Napoleon loved Russia so much that he tried to conquer it."

"Well, maybe he wanted to capture Russian art," Perez said. "As I understand it, he was pretty good at looting. Who knows what the French would have stolen from Mexico if Napoleon's nephew had succeeded in making Mexico a French colony."

Boris, shaking his head, said, "Let us give Francesco's question the respect it deserves. The French love light and its effects. We Russians live in a place where there is no sun for many months so we must invent light. Russian artists work with light even in the winter. One of my favorite paintings is in the Tretyakov in Moscow. It's by Igor Grabar. The subject is birch trees in the snow. It is as if he's scooped up all available winter light and used it to illuminate the trees."

"Tell us about this artist, Grabar. I don't know his work."

"Marc, you should visit Moscow. You would be perhaps surprised by the quality of the work in our museums. Grabar is in several collections in Moscow and his paintings are at the Hermitage in St. Petersburg. My point is that he taught art in Moscow and Leningrad. He was an expert in art restoration. Our partner, Sergei Androyov, has studied his writings and they will benefit us. One of the early Russian modernists whom the French loved was Konstantin Korovin. He won a gold medal for designing the Russian Pavilion at the 1900 World Fair held in Paris. Other Russian painters whose style and use of color made an impact in Paris in the late 1930s, a time that is important to us, include Martiros Saryan and abstract painters like Kasemir Malevich and Kandinsky, who lived in France after he left Germany to escape the Nazis. Finally, there is Ilia Dilinov, the young artist who took Paris by storm in 1939 and 1940 and who died at Stalingrad. He will be the focal point of one of our efforts. Marc knows of his work and reputation. We have a Kandinsky to sell and another one that with Sergei's help we have, shall I say, discovered and which we can sell once the authenticity of the first Kandinsky is established."

Libidoux, who had sat quietly taking in Boris's comments, nodded his head as Boris continued. "What you don't know, Marc, is that we have also discovered several unknown works by Dilinov. Perhaps even better than his painting that hangs in the d'Orsay. But we will discuss that when we meet again tomorrow, and we can also address your concern that someone will seize the inventory we have stored outside of Moscow."

◆　◆　◆

"I have a large house in Paris and yet we have to meet in this small hotel room in an out of the way area of the city I have never visited," grumbled Perez over croissants and coffee the next morning.

"Francesco," said Sofia, reaching across the low table to briefly put her hand over his, "it would be very unwise for all of us to be seen visiting your house or to meet again at Marc's gallery. And we are in the best suite in this little hotel. We are unlikely to be noticed here, and the hotel is convenient to a Metro station."

Shaking his head, Perez said, "I can't stand the metro with all those people crowding me. I am used to a car and a driver. I took a taxi this morning." Observing Sofia's disapproving look, he said, "I got out at the Lycée Molière and walked. I was careful. No one was following me." Boris stood up to fill his cup. "The French don't know how to make tea."

"Are you two done complaining so we can get to work?" Sofia said. "An open matter is Marc's worry about losing the art to some group in Moscow. Boris, explain our plan."

Thinking how Sofia was always focused on the present, Boris put his almost untouched tea down and continued to stand as he looked out the window to the Paris street scene below. Then he closed the blinds. "It would be prudent to move the art from Moscow. And to relocate Sergei since he needs to be able to access the paintings and will need a studio. Also, I am concerned about possible fallout from the L'affaire Petrov. He assured me that he had discussed the matter with no one, but unlikely as it seems, the Moscow police might actually investigate his unfortunate sauna accident."

"To where would you move the inventory?" asked Libidoux, still looking worried.

Pulling a map of Europe out of his jacket pocket, Boris spread it on the table and put a large thumb on a spot just below Dubrovnik. "This, Marc, is Montenegro, a beautiful country with a substantial Adriatic coast. Part of the former

Yugoslavia, it has become a favorite location for many Russians including some of Sofia's and my former colleagues. The coast is very picturesque—high bluffs overlooking the sea and many coves where small boats can land. I went there about four weeks ago and then invited Francesco to join me. We rented a villa outside of an old town called Budva. It has a small harbor and is on the road from Dubrovnik to the North, and more importantly, can be reached by highway from Belgrade, where there is a large airport and where many of our contacts reside and have influence.

"The paintings are now being flown to Belgrade. They will be discretely loaded on trucks, and brought to our villa.

"We have arranged for a very nice boat, owned by a Greek businessman who needs cash, will keep his mouth shut, and has an experienced crew to move the paintings to Venice. It's a one-day trip on this fast boat, arriving in Venice when the customs officials are anxious to get off work. From Venice, art can be transported to Paris, London, or shipped to New York."

"An audacious plan," said Libidoux, "but how will you get the paintings through Italian customs without creating a lot of attention?"

"A good question that we of course considered. Our original plan was to use Francesco's contacts in Italy to secure the cooperation of the Italian authorities, but we decided that such a course was not wise—we did not want to bring the Italians into this enterprise for several reasons."

"It was Sofia who solved our dilemma," observed Francesco.

"Yes, she flew from Moscow to Dubrovnik and spent a few days with us. There is an old inn outside of Budva where we stayed. It overlooks the Adriatic. We sat on the terrace and watched the *Argos*, our boat, come into the harbor. We went down, met the crew and inspected the boat. Very luxurious. Five guest cabins, a large main salon, hallways, a second salon on the upper deck—perfect for cruising the Mediterranean. After we came back to the inn, Sofia asked if we had noticed the numerous paintings hanging on the walls of the guest cabins, the two salons, the passageways and other spaces."

"I said of course I saw them but they were not very memorable. And she said, "That is the point." Sofia took up the explanation, "Over a period of several months we will make a number of cruises from Montenegro to Venice. Each time we enter Venetian waters, the customs inspectors will come on the boat. They will be looking for people without papers—merchandise, perhaps drugs—and they are unlikely to pay any attention to the paintings on the walls of the boat.

"On each Montenegro to Venice leg of the round trip we replace the boat's paintings with our paintings. When it arrives in Venice, the boat will dock along the canal on the Riva dei Sette Martiri close to Castello and Francesco's gallery. We move our paintings to his gallery, and the boat returns to Montenegro. We repeat the routine over, perhaps, two months. Then the paintings that were in Moscow will be in Venice, and we vacate the villa at Budva."

"Very clever. But Sergei and security in Montenegro?"

"Marc," said Boris, "the villa has a suitable space for a studio—great light. We will bring some men from Moscow to watch over the place. Sofia has already shot with them—they are former Spetsnaz—reliable—although they are not as good at shooting as Sofia—few people are. As for security in Venice, that will be up to Francesco. After all, he is about to become a gallery owner."

Francesco smiled. "Yes, I'm off to Venice. My real estate agent has found a location that meets my specifications and it will take only minor modifications to make it a suitable, if temporary, gallery. I'm bringing a colleague from Mexico City who has New York gallery experience to assist me."

"You have addressed my concerns," said Libidoux. "Now it's time to put our plan in action. I propose that we start with the Monet. You can ship it from Moscow to my gallery in Paris, treating it as a normal business transaction. As we have agreed, Francesco will finance my purchase of the Monet from the anonymous Russian collector with a loan of dollars, Euros, and pesos that he will deposit in my account. I will pay for the paintings by transferring Euros from my account to the Swiss account of the Russian collector's Swiss company. Boris and Sofia will then cause the Swiss company, protected by Swiss banking secrecy, to remit a portion of the Euros used to pay for the painting to Francesco, keeping the rest. After I sell the Monet, I will take a cut, repay the remainder of Francesco's loan and then he, Boris and Sofia will divide the balance."

"With some variations," Perez grinned, "this pattern will be repeated both in Paris and through my Venice gallery. Private transactions. Hard to trace funds transfers. Clean money. I love it!"

"Marc," said Boris, "the first stage in implementing our plan is the art auction coming up in a few weeks here in Paris. How are your preparations going?"

"The new gallery, Sidney Pebbles, has accepted the Monet, a Kandisky and some of the Dilinov works. This will be the gallery's opening auction, and there is a lot of buzz around it, here in Paris and beyond."

"Good," said Boris, as he got up from the table. "This is the kind of planning that Sofia and I are accustomed to from our former organization. I am off to Montenegro."

Chapter Sixteen

MARSEILLES

Marcos and Luis were back in Marseilles observing the unloading of another shipment of refrigerators. As two trucks left the port bound for Italy, two of the dockworkers who had unloaded the refrigerators motioned that they wanted to talk with the Mexicans. A third Mexican began translating into Spanish the comments of the two dockworkers. As the conversation grew heated, Luis said, "Gilberto, are they asking to be paid off?"

"*Si*, they claim that they have opened some of the refrigerators and they know what they contain."

"Tell them to fuck off. We are paying the customs inspectors and they are supposed to take care of anyone else."

"I told them that. They say that they are only getting small change from the inspectors and that when they complained, they were told to talk with us."

"And if we don't pay them?"

After a further discussion between Gilberto and the dockworkers, he turned to Luis, who said, "I think I got the gist of their response. The older one pointed to his shoulder—where the French cops wear their rank insignia. They are threatening to go to the police."

"*Exacto.*"

"Ask them how many others of the dockworkers know what is in the refrigerators?"

The two dockworkers stood with their hands on their hips facing the Mexicans and one of them had enough Spanish to say, "Only my brother."

The three Mexicans huddled for a moment and then Gilberto told the dockworkers that they did not have much money with them but that if the two of them and the brother would meet him and Luis early tomorrow morning they would bring 100,000 Euros. The dockworkers talked and said that they wanted 150,000 Euros—50,000 for each of them. After further discussion, Gilberto said to them, "Okay, but only this one payment."

The Frenchmen nodded and Luis, who had been looking around the area as Gilberto talked with the dockworkers, pointed to a corner of the dockyards where several large cranes and other pieces of equipment were parked. "Tell them you and I will be over there with the money at seven-thirty tomorrow morning. And tell them to bring the brother."

◆　◆　◆

The next morning there was a slight rain as Luis and Gilberto stood in the dockyard next to the cab of a large rusting crane. A canvas bag was at their feet. Three dockworkers sauntered over to them through the light fog.

Gilberto pointed to the canvas bag on the ground next to the crane. "Go ahead, open it up," Gilberto said. As the dockworkers bent over the bag, the door of the crane's cab above the men opened and Marcos reached out holding a silenced Nighthawk Enforcer .45 caliber pistol and fired three shots down into the heads of the dockworkers. Gilberto pulled out a similar weapon and placed two more bullets into each of their heads as they fell to the ground.

Luis then pulled on a pair of gloves and opened up a large switchblade knife. Pushing the dockworkers over on their backs, he pried out the eyes of each, placing the eyeballs in a plastic bag and motioned for Gilberto to pick up the canvas bag. Marcos climbed down from the crane and the Mexicans disappeared into the sea's early morning mist. Behind them seagulls screeched and flocked to the three bodies.

Chapter Seventeen

PARIS

Marc Libidoux knew this was a very important night for him and for the Paris art scene. It was a chance for him to finally reach the upper echelon of Paris dealers—and to make himself rich. But would their plan work? They had worked through it more than once. Even if it failed, and only the Monet sold, they would still have a win.

Libidoux thought of the other reason this night was important. If Sidney Pebbles' new auction house was successful, it just might join the ranks of Sothebys and Christies. If anyone could do it, Libidoux thought, it was Sidney Pebbles, one of the richest men in France and a major art collector. And Libidoux would have been there from the start.

The taxi turned off the Champs-Élysées onto the Rue Marbeuf, turned left and stopped in front of a white stone building with the name *Sidney Pebbles* discretely etched in a mantle above the door. Joining a busy scene of taxis and limousines discharging their passengers, Libidoux nodded to an acquaintance.

After stopping at a desk staffed by three slender young women who appeared to have been dressed by the famous fashion houses nearby, he greeted a number of dealers and collectors and entered the auction room.

In this, the inaugural auction of Sidney Pebbles, little had been spared to create the necessary environment to entice people to buy but also to reassure them that Sidney Pebbles would become a brand in the art world. *Most collectors,* thought Libidoux, *needed the security blanket of a brand—an auction house, a leading dealer or a famous collector, and I want to become such a brand.*

Libidoux walked into the auction hall, filled with rows of chairs that he heard had been designed by Christian Liagre to be comfortable but slightly tilted to keep bidders a bit on the edge of their seats. He couldn't see a tilt but he did wonder if they were designed to safely accommodate someone of his size.

He looked up at the second floor and the row of windows behind which bidders and consignors, who did not wish to mingle with the crowd, could sit, drink champagne and look at one of the screens around the room that translated each Euro bid into other currencies.

The room was beginning to fill up. The auctioneer was a Dane who Libidoux knew had previously worked in the United States. He was standing at the podium looking over some papers. Dressed in a black suit and a black tie, he projected understated elegance. To his right several of Pebbles' employees were standing, ready to begin their task of conveying bids they received over the phone. To the auctioneer's left, three of the paintings that were to be auctioned hung on the wall along with four more on easels. Libidoux strained to see if any of his works were among those displayed. He saw the Kandinsky on an easel but didn't see the Monet. The absence of the Monet from such a prime display was, he thought, an indication that their plan was working. An advisor to a wealthy Belgian family with whom Pebbles had dealt with on a few occasions and not particularly happily, came up next to him. "Well, do you think old Sidney can pull this off? Sotheby's and Christie's have been around for over 200 years, Harry Phillips' house for almost that long—although I think he now sells more jewelry and furniture than paintings."

Thinking to himself that referring to Harry Phillips as if he knew him, was typical of the brashness of this fellow. But before he could respond, the Belgian went on, "I hear that you are representing a collector with a couple of pieces in tonight's auction including a Monet. I am surprised they didn't put the Monet on the cover of the catalogue. The catalogue says it and your Ilia Dilinov and your Kandinsky are from a Russian collection. That is not much provenance."

Libidoux stared down at the Belgian whose face reminded him of a ferret and was about to say something unpleasant to him when one of the auction house employees handed him a note. After reading it, Libidoux walked off following the employee, saying over his shoulder, "You are right; that is what the catalogue says."

Entering a small conference room on the second floor, Libidoux was met by a tall man wearing a blue suit and a quiet necktie, and frowning at a small file he held in his hand. Marc recognized him as the director of the auction house.

"Mr. Libidoux, we may have a problem that we should discuss."

"And what is the nature of this problem, Mr. Bastelle?"

"My associate, Madame Letto, will explain the concern," he said, pointing to a stocky woman in her fifties wearing a not very stylish grey suit, no-nonsense black shoes, with hair pulled back into a severe bun. She reminded Libidoux of his gym teacher in Lyon, a class that held few positive memories for him. The man continued, "Madame Letto is in charge of reviewing the authenticity and provenance of works we put on auction. You may know of her as she was at the Musée d'Orsay for a number of years."

Libidoux bowed slightly. "Charmed, Madame."

"Mr. Libidoux," she said briskly, "this auction house will distinguish itself from its competitors by examining the authenticity and provenance of all work we put up for auction."

"I thought all the major auction houses subject the work they auction to such scrutiny."

"Not always effectively. Many of us who were at the Christie's auction of the Chagall painting *Les Maries Au Bouquet De Fleurs* thought it was not genuine, but Christie's sold it and," a thin smile appeared, "of course, it was a fake."

"Did you tell Christie's of your concern before the auction?"

"Mr. Libidoux, I was not employed by Christie's. Now, you have told us that you are representing a Russian collector who wishes to remain anonymous. So, we subjected your paintings to extra scrutiny. We used black light, x-ray and pigment analysis on each of the three works."

Libidoux visibly stiffened.

"We are convinced that they are genuine. The Monet is listed in the Monet catalogue raisonné and the Kandinsky has equally solid documentation. There is no catalogue raisonné for the works of Ilia Dilinov. Unfortunately, the Dilinov expert in Paris is out of the country. However, I personally compared your painting with the Dilinov at the d'Orsay and I am satisfied with it. So, our concern is not with authenticity, but with the provenance of the Monet and the Kandinsky."

Libidoux was relieved but still tense. "The Kandinsky was in the collection of a Dutch dealer but disappeared during the war. We are not aware of any member of the dealer's family surviving the war and claiming ownership of the art stolen from him. The Monet was seized by the Nazis from a Jewish family living in Paris. We understand that there may be family members living in New York."

"The only provenance you have provided, Mr. Libidoux," said Madame Letto, "are sales documents signed by an official of the Russian government transferring ownership of the Monet and the Kandinsky to the Swiss corporation you represent. Are you asserting that the paintings were taken by the Soviet Army at the end of the war?"

Libidoux grew anxious again. "I do not know how they came into the Russian government's possession, but your surmise is reasonable. Madame Letto, I'm sure you know that in 1946 the Soviet Military Administration issued an order to the effect that art liberated by the Red Army that had previously been stolen by the Nazis was the property of the Soviet Union. This principle was later codified by the Russian Duma. So, the provenance of these paintings now begins anew with possession by the Russian government."

"Mr. Libidoux," interjected Bastelle, "those Russian claims of ownership are not widely accepted in the west. Should the survivors of the French family that owned the Monet bring a legal action, they could well prevail. Your description of the chain of ownership of the painting might hold up, or it might not, but we don't want to begin our history as a world-class auction house with a dispute over ownership of a painting. The Monet, while authentic, is too well-known to auction because it is likely that its sale will be well publicized, and lead to difficulties."

"What about a private sale?" Libidoux said, sounding only slightly desperate.

"Perhaps later we can discuss a private sale. Your owner could consign it to us. We know of several collectors who would be interested in buying the painting. Everything about such a transaction would be private. But for now it cannot be in the auction. I am sorry. We should have had this discussion earlier. We would like to have a fruitful relationship with you and your client, but we must ask you to take the Monet back. The Kandinsky can remain in the auction."

Libidoux got up and paced around the room wringing his hands. Finally, he said, "I submit to your decision, but I ask that you do one thing for me as part of our ongoing business relationship. Will you please make it known that the Monet is being withdrawn, not over questions of authenticity, and that you have in fact concluded that it is authentic, but at the seller's choice."

"We can do that," said Bastelle.

"*Merci*, Monsieur Bastelle." He turned to Madame Letto and bowed.

Libidoux returned to the auction room and took a seat to the auctioneer's right, eight rows back. "These chairs aren't very comfortable," said a stocky bald man who sat down next to Libidoux.

"Hello, Alexandre," said Libidoux. "I am glad to see you here. With your client list, you provide credibility to this auction."

"Oh, I am just here to observe and see how Sidney gets this enterprise off the ground. But I do have my phone with me—just in case."

The auctioneer welcomed the participants as the Pebbles' employees took their places to his right in a semicircle. He then announced that two works listed in the catalogue would not be in the auction.

"So, your Monet will not be auctioned, Marc. I looked for you at the party last night because I have a client who might be interested in it, but I wanted to get some sense of the price range your collector has in mind."

"Alexandre, I would be glad to discuss the Monet with you."

"I saw this Dane handle an auction in New York. He is good—very smooth and seems to be able to hold the interest of people over a long period of time. The estimate on the first work, the Giacometti piece, seems low. What do you think?"

"Well, they want to start with a low estimate and then sell it above the estimate to create an atmosphere early on of a successful auction." After several paintings were sold, Alexandre turned to Libidoux, "Now the real action starts. This Picasso is a small canvas but it is a beauty. What do you think the reserve is?"

"I heard it was seventy-five percent—so they will pull it if they don't get about eight million Euros."

"Hmm. Well, someone just raised their paddle at six

million. Probably not a real bid."

"They have to start somewhere."

The auctioneer said, "Do I hear seven million? Thank you, madame," he said to a woman sitting to Libidoux's left.

"There aren't many Picassos out there of this quality, ladies and gentlemen. Do I hear nine million?" A paddle went up from someone Alexandre said was a proxy.

"Madame, what about nine-and-a-half million? Thank you."

"Do I hear ten million?" A paddle went up from near the front.

"Who is that?" asked Marc.

"Alexandre responded, "I think he represents a Chinese buyer, but he could also be bidding on behalf of the Rolf Gallery in London. They sold a Picasso last month."

"Alexandre, you are surely well connected."

"That is my job."

Turning to the proxy, the auctioneer said—"eleven million?"

He waited patiently while the woman who was bidding for the anonymous buyer talked on her phone. She then raised the paddle.

Pointing at the woman sitting near Libidoux, he said, "Madame, will you go to eleven-and-a-half?" The woman shook her head no. "Then this beautiful painting won't be yours. What about you, sir? Okay, thank you. We now have eleven-and-a-half million Euros. Is there someone out there who is lying in the weeds? This is your chance, Madame; do you want to come back in at twelve million? No? What about you sir? Do we have twelve million?"

The room was quiet. The bidder near the front was on his cell phone. He raised his paddle. Turning again to his left the auctioneer addressed the proxy, "Will you bid twelve-and-a-half?"

More silence. Then a head shaking no.

"Do I hear twelve-and-a-half for this great painting?"

More silence. "Okay, sold for twelve million Euros. Congratulations sir. You have purchased a fine work."

The auction continued and when the Dilinov and the Kandinsky had been sold, Libidoux left the auction house and called Boris who was in Venice.

"Boris, it went just as I hoped it would. The Dilinov sold at a nice price, as did the Kandinsky, and the auction house put out the word that the Monet is authentic but that it is being withdrawn for other reasons."

"Excellent, please wire the funds as we have agreed. Congratulations, your bona fides as a source of authentic art are established. With the Dilinov sold, we can now proceed on the plan for you to do a Dilinov show at your gallery. Sergei will bring some of his paintings to Paris. Let me know if your Japanese client is still interested in a Klee."

After completing his call to Boris, Libidoux walked almost in a daze away from the Rue de la Trémoille, winding his way through the prosperous neighborhood of shops, flats and small restaurants. He was oblivious to the traffic.

What have I just done? he asked himself. *Did I finally take the step away from being a small time art dealer. Can I carry this through?*

He paused on the Pont de l'Alma to look at the colored lights of the boats below him as they reflected off the water. Then as he walked along the Avenue de New York, he heard a voice just behind him over his left shoulder.

"It sounds as if everything went according to plan. Doesn't always happen that way. Good work."

He snapped out of his reverie with such a sharp jolt that his neck hurt. He turned and recognized Sofia in a long black-hooded cloak, her face partly hidden in the folds of her hood.

"You startled me."

"You were so deep in thought that I worried you were going to get hit by a car when you crossed the avenue near the bridge."

"I never noticed."

"According to Boris, you did well at the auction."

"Yes, we exceeded the estimate on the Kandinsky and did better than expected on the Dilinov."

"I am surprised that you didn't stay until the end."

"I wanted to make them think that I was disappointed that they pulled the Monet—actually I was sweating too much to stay around."

"Never pulled off anything this big?"

"Nothing with this potential."

"Well, with the Monet at least you had a real original. You can sell the painting through Sidney Pebbles, and Sergei is completing a copy of another Monet that disappeared during the war. He has a photo to work from. A private buyer will pay a lot for it—it is a beautiful landscape. He chose this Monet because he thinks it will bring a high price. Boris agreed with him—I think he was surprised that Sergei had such a keen knowledge of the Monet prices."

They had walked partly around the Place Trocadero, dodging an increasing number of pedestrians as well as cars. They moved patiently, sometimes talking, sometimes silent. At one point Libidoux said, "Sergei seems to know a lot about the art market."

Sofia replied, "He appears to me to be above that—caring only about painting."

Sofia gently took Libidoux's elbow and guided him along the Avenue Raymond Poincare toward the Place Victor Hugo which he could see at the end of the wide street which climbed away from the river. Suddenly, Sofia noticed him sag, and he became heavier on her arm. "Marc, you have had a stressful time. Stop and catch your breath. There is a bistro a few steps away. We can sit down and get something to eat and drink."

They walked into a room decorated with tiles painted with colorful abstract designs, and Libidoux sank heavily into a soft banquette letting out a grunt as he sat down. Sofia ordered two glasses of champagne. "After all, we have something to celebrate."

After tasting his champagne, Libidoux said, "Sofia, were you following me?"

"Not at all. But I was standing outside Sidney Pebbles when you left. You seemed a bit disoriented. Boris phoned me after you talked with him and was concerned about you. Do you know that you collided with two people on the street and almost got struck by a car as you crossed the Avenue New York at the Place de L'Alma?"

"Thanks for looking after me. I sometimes do get distracted."

"With the work we will be doing, you will need to be aware of your surroundings—no day dreaming—it could be very dangerous."

"Marc, let me ask you a question. Do you ever have qualms about selling art that is not authentic?"

As he contemplated her question, he looked at her and realized how little he knew about her. She was lovely he knew, but her eyes were so cold.

"An interesting question. Do you?" he asked.

She stared at him and said, "Qualms are not in my nature. I sell things that people want to buy. As Boris would put it, what we do is manipulate the concept of value. There are thousands of artists out there. I have studied many, so have you. Boris has an encyclopedic memory and could name numbers of excellent painters who have never reached market acceptance. If someone considers the work of such artists beautiful, who determines its value?"

"Buyers are the last people on the food chain who determine value," said Libidoux. "The auction houses and big-name dealers are way ahead of them, as are the most famous collectors. They create value. They are themselves a brand."

"Marc, you want to be one of those dealers, right?"

"Of course." Libidoux seemed to regain his excitement from earlier. "The winning lottery ticket is to be someone like Ambroise Vollard or Joseph Duveen. They anointed the artist. They sold work of the artist they acquired pre-anointment, or acted as a middleman. Leo Castelli perfected this skill in the middle of the last century. Gagosian and several others in London and New York now practice it. I hope that we can add Paris to that list—perhaps with an allied outpost in Venice."

Libidoux thought to himself that she well understood the business and asked, "Do you think that Sidney Pebbles can become a brand?"

"I don't know. He has the money and the connections. Paris should be a commercial center for art, like London and New York. After all, museums give credibility to an artist by buying or showing their work, and Paris museums are certainly on a level with New York or London. But only recently have they started to become as aggressive in showing the work of new artists."

Libidoux wiped his forehead and said, "For our enterprise, though, the market is pre-World War II art. The world was in turmoil. Provenance was not as methodical. Photography less effective in capturing a painting. And a photograph in black-and-white from, say, 1938 will not be good enough for even an expert to determine if a painting is the original or a fake."

Libidoux took a gulp from his wine glass and continued, "What is a fake? Artists like Rubens or Rembrandt didn't work alone in glorious, creative isolation. They had studios with assistants who worked on the Master's paintings. Some of their assistants were, in effect, specialists—all they did were heads, or landscape backgrounds. Maybe the major brushstrokes were the Masters, or they did the layers of glaze, and they certainly did the signatures—but were these paintings originals?"

Libidoux poured himself another glass of wine. "How many Rembrandts were painted in his studio with only minimal input from him? Who knows? The same for many highly acclaimed moderns: Picasso, Monet, Giacometti, furniture makers, sculptors. Many collectors know or suspect they own fakes but don't want to admit it. How embarrassing. The same for museums. Most of the time when I am asked to evaluate a work for authenticity, the owners want me to say yes, even if no or uncertain is the answer. It's all in the names of the artists. I can give you examples of well-known artists who make copies of earlier works by lesser-known—but still known—artists and the copy sells for more than the original. Even major artists do copies that they are proud of. Why, the famous British artist Turner did a painting based on an earlier work by Claude Lorrain hanging in the National Gallery in London. Turner gave his painting to the same museum, but he required that it hang next to the Lorrain original. So, qualms, no. My criterion is that the fake be really good. Then it is a work of art, is it not?"

He didn't wait for Sofia to answer.

"Take Rembrandt, for example. What greater pleasure is there for a collector than to own an original Rembrandt? Yet how many do you think exist?"

Sofia shook her head no, thinking *he is really wound up but maybe this venting will relieve some of the pressure he has been under leading up to the auction. I will let him go on for a bit longer then put him in a taxi to his apartment.*

"Well, no one knows for sure. When the first scholarly effort to catalogue his work was started early in the twentieth century, it was estimated that there were over 700 Rembrandts in museums and private collections. That early cataloging work reduced the number to under 600. Today, it's estimated that there are well under 400 actual Rembrandts. Think of all the people who discovered that their priceless painting wasn't so priceless. It turned out that some of the Rembrandts owned by the Queen of England were not by his hand. A national tragedy for the British and that nice lady, the Queen. I am sure she was heartbroken. Unnecessary anguish.

Was her *Bust of a Young Man in a Turban* now less beautiful because a committee concluded that it was painted by one of Rembrandt's apprentices and not by the master? Was the pleasure in the painting or in the snobbishness of owning it?"

"If your Mr. Sergei is as good as he seems to be, his work will give viewers great pleasure."

"Yes," said Sofia, "and the more they pay for his work, the greater the pleasure, right?"

Libidoux nodded, "Like your jewelry business. A reputable dealer, beautiful pieces, high prices—happy customers who wouldn't even consider the thought that the piece was not genuine."

"Perhaps. Now, Marc, pay the bill and let's get taxis. You need to go back to your place and unwind. You will have an important visitor tomorrow."

Chapter Eighteen

PARIS

Sergei Androyov sat quietly in Marc Libidoux's conference room, clutching a black battered portfolio under one arm. Sofia stood next to the door, thinking how thin and pale he was. His white skin standing out against his black hair and beard, and his fingers so long. Sofia said to herself that someone seeing him on the street would guess that he was a violinist, always wearing a black sweater and pants and with unkempt hair.

Libidoux bent over the two drawings laying on his table ,shining a sharp beam of light on them.

"So, the one with the green lines is yours, the other—the cream one with the dancing figure—from the Moscow inventory?"

Sergei nodded.

Libidoux pulled two books from a case at the end of the room and opened one of them. After looking at the two drawings and holding them up to the photos in his books, he said, "The abstract dancing figure is in the Klee book. Your drawing with the more pronounced green vertical lines is not. Although one very similar is. When he was at the Bauhaus, Klee would work on several paintings at the same time. So a lot of his work, at least superficially, looks similar. My Qatar client very much wants a Klee. He is not concerned about provenance—he is in the market for a work no matter how it was acquired—but he will probably have some authentication done. Tell me how you made the green lines drawing. The dancer drawing could sell here or in Venice although there may well be an issue over provenance since it was once in the collection of an Austrian Jewish businessman. But we will see. Like with the Monet, we can leverage a dispute over provenance into credibility for our anonymous Russian collector. Pebbles' local competitor, Christie's Paris, had a Klee at auction recently that sold nicely."

Observing the scene from the doorway, Sofia said, "But how will you explain to your client the absence of the green lines drawing from the Klee Catalogue Raisonné?"

"Boris and I discussed this in Moscow when we decided to paint this picture," observed Sergei. "The picture of the dancer was done by Klee in 1939, shortly before he died." Pointing to the green lines drawing, he said, "This one is very similar and was done with comparable materials. You see in the upper right-hand corner where it's signed, it's dated 1939. We'll say that it was kept by his family after his death. He was a banned artist then in Germany. There was no art market elsewhere in Europe so they kept it. It remained in private hands until after 2004 when the catalogue was published."

"Sounds good, Sergei," said Libidoux, "and I'll give the buyer a discount."

"That will make him happy," said Sofia.

"Sergei, please, continue discussing your technique," said Libidoux, clearly fascinated.

"Well, it's a work on paper. Klee often worked on paper then used glue to affix the paper to cardboard. The paper was fairly easy to find. I have a lot of old books for this reason and I removed a blank page of the right size from a book published in Hungary in 1938. The paper will pass analysis because it's actually old. Finding the right cardboard was harder but Klee used ordinary materials and this piece is cut from a box used to ship clothing in the 1930s. Glue was not hard. Hide glue was used frequently in that time and I got some in powder form, matched the color to this work and then prepared it by mixing it with cold water, letting it stand and then heating it to the consistency I wanted.

"I mixed water colors with paste, used brushes from the 30s and went to work."

Looking intently at the drawing, Libidoux said, "But there are ink lines in your drawing and they look old and uneven, like the cream drawing."

"Yes, there are various ways to age ink. For really old drawings, it's very time-consuming. You have to deposit the ink unevenly, use a sharpened quill and sulphuric acid and heat to create the unevenness that is characteristic of very old ink on paper.

"With this drawing, I simply mixed the ink with water and let it evaporate back to its pre-mixed strength. But once evaporated, ink is not smooth and its granularity will make it look old when it is examined under magnification."

"Sergei, you impress me," said Libidoux. "You are all Boris said you were. Where are you off to now?"

"First, I will visit some shops and buy some old books and canvasses. Maybe some brushes if I can find them. I will also visit a few galleries. I don't know much about the business side of art—values, markets, that kind of thing—maybe I will learn something more on this visit. Then I will fly to Belgrade and drive to the villa. All the art is now either in Montenegro or in Venice. I will go to Montenegro to work. I will be in Venice to celebrate the opening of Galeria Perez. You should receive several Dilinov pieces shortly. See if you can tell which are Dilinovs and which are Sergeis," he said with a shy smile. And then he was gone.

He is like a wraith, thought Sofia, *and so simple.*

Chapter Nineteen

"Gerard, you're staring at me."

"Catherine, I am not staring, I am admiring your beautiful form. I have missed you and I repeat what I said at the airport yesterday. Welcome to Paris."

"Since the only part of Paris I have seen since I got here is your bedroom, I am looking forward to a long Saturday morning walk and some breakfast. I will unpack."

"My friends will be surprised that you are living here with me because they always said that I had so many clothes that no woman could live here because there was no room for her things."

"Your housekeeper did a good job of putting away the things I sent over. I am going minimalist so I can add to my wardrobe here."

"As I recall, you did pretty well in that regard when you were last in Paris."

She kissed him and said, "Okay, mister policeman, let's shower and take a walk."

They walked along the Rue St. Louis around the Notre Dame and into the heart of Paris's left bank. They were hand-in-hand as Gerard guided her into a small church. "This is Saint-Julien-le-Pauvre," he said, "a counterpoint to Notre Dame and a place that is part of an old love story, that of Heloise and Abelard."

"I remember something about that. They were lovers who were separated and never allowed to reunite. But they continued to write letters to each other, very romantic letters, for many years."

"Very good, my dear."

"You would be surprised what a girl from Wisconsin knows about French romance, even if it was hundreds of years ago. But what is their connection to this church?"

"Abelard was a philosopher who taught at Notre Dame in the twelfth century. I suppose today you would call him a radical. He left Notre Dame and a number of his followers left with him to set up a center of learning in this church which is as old as Notre Dame. So, while I doubt that Heloise ever set foot in St. Julien, its history is intertwined with hers and Abelard's."

As they left the church, Catherine stopped and commented on the painters bent over their easels who lined the small square. "It's so beautiful here," she said.

"Yes, the view of Saint-Séverin from here is a popular one to paint and to photograph. Some would say it's quintessential Paris—but I don't think there is such a thing."

As they strolled through the narrow winding streets of the old Latin Quarter and then turned back toward the Seine, Catherine noticed that Gerard had turned quiet, and asked, "What are you thinking about?"

"Oh, I was reflecting on how many times I have walked these streets. This was my neighborhood when I grew up, since we lived on the Île Saint-Louis. I know every alley and building. My friends and I pretended we were French Resistance fighters ambushing Nazis. Now I am here with you, and my life has taken a new turn."

Catherine smiled. "Tell me more about your neighborhood, Gerard."

"Much has happened on these streets over the history of this city. My mother told me of the barricades that the people of Paris built here during their fight to liberate Paris from the Germans during August of 1944."

They crossed the Boulevard Saint-Michel and Gerard commented, "There were barricades on the Quai des Grands-Augustins to prevent the Germans from moving tanks along the river, and on the Boulevard Saint-Germain."

"And your mother witnessed the fighting?"

"Oh, yes. She even took a few pictures of the big barricade on the quai. They were grainy, but I remember in the picture overturned trucks, paving stones, furniture, anything people could find to build barricades."

"The occupation must have been hard on her."

"She didn't talk too much about it, but she and my sister, who was very young, both remembered how hungry they were. There was very little food in Paris in 1943 and 1944. She was afraid to move around much because the Germans watched her."

"Because of your father?"

"Yes, they knew he was with de Gaulle in London, and I'm sure they suspected her of passing messages to the Resistance."

"Did she?"

"As I have told you, my father admired Resistance people greatly and hated the French police and other collaborators."

"Your mother shared his views?"

"My mother shared his views. And in a very real way, what I do now, a career in police work, is a result of my father's feeling about the German occupation of Paris and how the French authorities responded. History has a long reach, and that history is now part of who I am."

They decided to stop for a coffee on the Boulevard Saint-Germain. Taking a seat on the terrace of a café, Gerard said, "This place, Café Les Deux Magots, also is part of the history of the uprising against the Germans."

Catherine said, "I know it was a favorite haunt of Hemingway, Gertrude Stein and that whole crowd of American expatriates living in Paris during the 20s and 30s."

"That's right. And that's why so many tourists come here. Perhaps they think they are channeling Hemingway or Fitzgerald. But for me it has another much more personal significance." He sipped his coffee and looked around.

"Are you going to tell me what?" smiled Catherine as she reached across the table and put her hand over his.

"By August 1944, this neighborhood was pretty much controlled by the Resistance. There were collaborators and Nazi agents of course, but as you have seen the streets here are narrow and winding. Much as they were in medieval times. The Germans kept their tanks in the Luxembourg gardens because they didn't want to maneuver them through these streets where they could be blocked and attacked or where people could serve Molotov cocktails to them from above. So it was a relatively safe place for Resistance types to meet. And one of the places they met was here."

"But what of the personal significance?"

"Just before the French and Americans entered Paris, my mother got a message to meet someone at a specific time the next morning at this café. The message was delivered by a young boy—Marcel Lefour."

"You have told me about him. He is the old man who loves escargot and who gets you information about the Paris underworld."

"Yes. Well, my mother came to the café and sitting over there," he pointed to a table along the back wall, "was a man wearing a straw hat and reading a newspaper. It was my father." Gerard seemed to be looking at him. "She hadn't seen him in four years. He had slipped into Paris the day before as one of de Gaulle's liaisons to the Resistance. He couldn't come to the apartment because it was being watched."

"Wow. That must have been a bittersweet reunion."

"Yes, the emotions of each must have been strong."

"Together, but not together. How hard that must have been."

"But he was able to come home a few days later when the Germans surrendered Paris, and I'm sure they then had a joyous reunion."

"Why's that?"

"I was born nine months later."

"And now you and I are here, sitting in the same café, but under very different circumstances."

"Yet drinking the same overpriced coffee." They laughed.

Looking across the small round table at Gerard, Catherine said, "I still can't quite believe that I am here with you and assigned to our Paris office."

"Well, you are here. I am happy, although I suppose we will need some cooking utensils."

"Yes, we will. Your reheating days are over. I am going to cook up a storm here."

"But, you will also be working hard—n'est ce pas?"

"Yes, Gerard. I will be working, not remodeling your apartment. As Nick Reschio said, the Paris office is a mess. They can't seem to close an investigation. I read a memo on the plane about two new cases—one a fire that nobody seems to know how it started and an expensive painting that the owner is making a claim on because it was stolen, but both his chain of ownership and provenance on the painting are shaky."

"Your Harvard art history major, all those lectures at MOMA and your New York gallery prowling should serve you in good stead."

"Art authentication claims are not my favorites. Everyone lies. It's somewhat like Sofia Mostov's fake jewels, the owners claim they are real but when proven to be fakes, they want a premium refund and to keep the jewels because their friends think they are real. But I'm anxious to get to work and to get to know Paris with you. I have even arranged to take French lessons over lunch."

"*Bon.* But I will teach you some French words that won't be in your lessons."

"Why you sexy fellow. But enough of this. How do you say it—badinage?—let's go shopping. I need some clothes."

Early that same evening, Gerard was changing for a dinner with Catherine at an old bistro on the Rue de Charonne not far from the Place des Vosges, when his phone rang. He looked at the name of the caller and answered.

"This cannot be good news, can it?"

"Well, it wasn't for the three Marseilles dockworkers who were killed this morning in the port," said Pierre. "Your hope that the Marseilles-Italy link would not heat up is, I am afraid, dashed."

"How can you be sure?" said Gerard.

"How can anyone be sure of anything in this murky business, but they were shot with a .45 caliber weapon, the same as the two Italians last month, and their eyes were cut out."

After a few moments of silence, Gerard said, "Can you go to Marseilles with me tomorrow morning?"

"Of course."

"Call down there and have them arrange to meet us. And please tell your former colleagues to secure the crime scene properly this time."

Chapter Twenty

A tall Marseilles detective, wearing a trenchcoat and with a stooped over posture, stood in the Marseilles dockyards, facing Pierre and Gerard.

"Thank you for coming down here for the day, Senior Inspector de Rochenoir and Detective Abou. It is a pleasure to meet you Senior Inspector, and to work with someone of your reputation."

"You are very kind, detective, but the work on this investigation has all been done by your former colleague, Detective Abou."

The Marseilles detective bowed slightly in Pierre's direction. "Inspector Monsey is in a meeting, but he asked me to accompany the two of you."

Standing next to a stack of shipping containers in the middle of the huge dockyards, Gerard said, "Let me summarize the facts as I understand them. There have been five murders here in the past several weeks. Two Italians, who we are told by the Italian police are from the Naples mob, and three dockworkers. All shot in the head with a .45 caliber weapon, one of which was found at the scene of the first murder."

"Yes, the three dockworkers were shot in the top of the head and then again while lying on the ground."

"And their eyes were gouged out," Pierre added.

"A very brutal crime," the Marseilles detective said. "I suppose it was some kind of message—'see nothing.' But who was the message for?"

"The other dockworkers and anyone else who might see," mused Pierre.

Gerard said, "The victims were first shot from a height perhaps from the cab of that crane, right?"

"Correct, Senior Inspector. Our reconstruction people think that the shooter was above them and shot down."

"Any prints or other evidence in the cab?"

"No."

"These are clearly professionals," said Gerard. "Like the first murders, there were extra shots for certainty."

The Marseilles detective nodded, and Pierre asked, "What have you learned from your questioning of dockworkers and others here in the port?"

"This port is, like most, somewhat of a law onto itself. The unions enforce discipline. There are pay-offs. There is a premium on no disruptions and always suspicion of outsiders. Particularly suspicion of the police, so we have not gotten much information yet."

"Pierre's report on the first two murders mentions that a freighter from Mexico docked in Marseilles the day before. Were there any Mexican ships in port when the second killings took place?"

"I don't know, Senior Inspector."

Gerard held up a document. "Well, we know. There was a Mexican ship in port the day before the murders."

The detective looked embarrassed.

"How much notice does the port get before a freighter arrives?"

"I don't know, Senior Inspector, but I can find out."

"Thank you. Also, please redouble your interviewing of people who were in the port at the time of the

murders. It's a busy place. Someone must have seen something. Maybe recognized someone from the time of the
earlier murders."

"Yes, Senior Inspector."

"We have reviewed the medical examiner's report, the customs inspector's report, and the crime scene. And now that
we have talked with you, we will catch the TGV back to Paris.
You have been most helpful, detective. Give our regards to
Inspector Monsey."

Settling into their seats on the bullet train, Pierre turned
to Gerard, "You see what I mean about the Marseilles police?
And Monsey more or less snubbed us."

"They aren't exactly acting as if these murders are a
high priority. Perhaps they think we'll solve the case for
them. Are you thinking what I am about the port inspector's reports?"

"You mean the cargo?"

"Yes, Pierre. Preceding each of the murders, a ship from
Mexico docked at Marseilles. And the cargo manifestos show
that there were shipments of refrigerators each time. Let's
look at all shipments into Marseilles from Mexico for the past
twelve months and see if the cargo included refrigerators or
any other items from the same shipper."

Pierre stroked his chin and said, "The inspector's report
is pretty thin. It doesn't indicate where the cargo was going,
only that it was loaded on trucks. We need to know the destination of those trucks. The license numbers are on the report.
And they are Italian trucks. I will check with the border police
and see what I can find out."

"Tomorrow we'll send two of our people down there to
work with the locals to interview various port workers and
officials. Make sure they've checked hotels, the train station
and the like."

"Monsey will whine about it," Pierre commented.

"One word from him, Pierre, and I'll make clear to him

that my next conversation will be with my old friend, the Marseilles Chief. Once we get some more information I should have a conversation with my new friend, Steffani Terzazo."

Chapter Twenty-One

"Boris, today this Mexican is happy!"

Seated at the head of a large table in a small osteria, a short distance east of the Campo Bandiera e Moro, Francesco Perez was beaming. Around the table sat Boris Voroshilov, Sofia Mostov, and Sergei Androyov.

"My Italian gallery opens tonight with some wonderful pieces that are already creating a buzz in Venice. My colleague from New York said that even some important American collectors are coming. You and Marc have selected excellent work for my first show. The Diego Rivera will draw many who have not seen an original of his work. There are young artists working in this area, so we should get the Biennale crowd if we have done a good job of promotion." Francesco raised his glass. "To promotion!" he toasted. After clinking and sips, he said with some pride, "Sofia, how do you like my new neighborhood? You wanted us to locate the gallery close to the arsenale and to the canal. Castello is away from most of the other galleries in San Marco."

"Is there *anything* it's close to?" asked Sofia sarcastically.

"Well, it's very close to this restaurant and to my favorite Venetian church."

"And which one is that, Francesco?" asked Sofia.

"You can't see it from here but it's on the other side of the canal just over there," he gestured toward the arsenale. "It's the Church of San Martino—maybe not so beautiful—but beside the door there is a lion statue and Venetians—always a conspiratorial group—used to denounce their fellow citizens by slipping a message into the mouth of the lion. They call it the Bocca de Leone—the mouth of the lion. I want to bring a lion like that to Mexico City—it will make the work of my associates much more efficient." He laughed and raised his glass again. "To business and to the beautiful woman at my table."

"Francesco, you have had too much wine," Sofia said. "But I admit you have a location in a place that's not easy to find. Perhaps that will add to its cachet."

"Yes, I am happy, but please eat. The food at this little place is exceptional. Yesterday I had ravioli stuffed with lobster in fish sauce; Luigi had duck breast with plums and leeks. Try the branzino baked in salt—very Venetian."

"How is it prepared?"

"Boris, the whole fish—a sea bass—is cooked on the bone. It is—how would you say it in English—juicy. And the white wines from this region are flavorful and complex."

"Francesco, you are becoming an Italian. But let's talk about your show.

"There was an article today in *Il Gazzettino* about it," said Sofia.

"*Il Gazzettino* is a widely-read newspaper published in Venice," beamed Francesco.

"And what did the article say?" asked Boris.

"Well, it described Dilinov's work as," Francesco paused, "infused with light and color—*luce e colore.*"

"Francesco, you not only now can read Italian, you are speaking it," praised Boris.

"Of course, Boris. I'm a man of many talents. The article also noted that Dilinov has a painting in the collections of the Musée d'Orsay in Paris and the Tretyakov in Moscow, as well as in the collections of two well-known Russian industrialists.

And it said that there would be a showing of these artists at a Paris gallery, following the Venice opening. So we are building some momentum."

"Did the article mention other artists that will be in the show?"

"Yes, the more I paid the reporter, the more notes he took."

"The reporter interviewed you?"

"Of course."

"And you paid him?"

"He has a family to support."

"I talked and my assistant Luigi translated. I told him that there would be works by Kandinsky, Monet, Picasso, and Paul Klee in the show, as well as additional Russian artists—Martiros Saryan, Chaim Soutine, Aleksandr Yakovlev, and Anton Yevgeny, who, along with Dilinov, was part of the 1938-1939 Paris art scene."

The reporter took a picture of me standing between the Dilinov and Yevgeny paintings and quoted me as saying that their deaths in World War II were heroic. The picture is in the article."

"Francesco, how do you know their deaths were heroic? I read somewhere that Dilinov died of pneumonia."

"Boris, artists who died heroically sell better than artists who die in bed."

"Probably true. But do you think it wise to have so much attention on you?"

"Why not? I am important in Mexico. Now I will become important in Italy."

Perez motioned for the waiter and ordered sardines and an assortment of meats and olives as an appetizer, along with a Colli Berici sparkling white wine. "This is a local wine. And from this maker, quite good."

"How many pieces do you expect to sell?" asked Sofia.

"Ah, Sofia, for you it's always about money," said Perez.

"Sofia always gets quickly to the heart of things," said

Boris, "and for her the heart is almost always money."

"Charming as you all are," she said, "I'm not here for the pleasure of your company."

"Besides the pieces we'll sell," said Perez, "I've also arranged to loan a couple of our paintings on very favorable terms."

Sergei, who had been sitting quietly said, "Loans—I have never heard of loaning a painting."

"Sergei, it's a form of banking that I've discussed with Boris and Sofia."

"Loans. Banking. You are all beyond me. I just paint."

"Okay, Sergei, I will explain," offered Francesco. "You are soon going to be rich. You will probably invest some of your money in corporate stock. You no longer get a stock certificate. Your broker, who will probably be affiliated with a bank, makes an electronic transfer. You get a report. But your stock is not passive. Your broker will very likely loan it to an institution that needs it for collateral for a short-term transaction. The broker gets compensated for the loan and then the stock is electronically put back in your account. Well, Sergei, why not do the same with paintings?" Francesco gestured as if it were inarguable. "Particularly those where provenance issues make it hard to sell them at auction—or where the painting is not authentic but one of your brilliant forgeries—for example a Gauguin that was confiscated by the Nazis and has never turned up. The painting looks authentic. But descendants of the owners from whom it was stolen or the Israeli government would come after us if we tried to sell it at auction or even through a dealer if word of the transaction leaked out. So the transaction would have to be kept confidential. But say we have customers—and I have several in this situation—who need large amounts of money for a short time to buy, let us say, valuable items: drugs or arms, for example, that they can quickly sell. They borrow the money from a high-interest lender who operates off the radar and give the lender one of your paintings as collateral along with some provenance—which we may have created. They buy the items, resell them, and repay the lender who returns the painting to them. We charge a high fee or a percentage of the deal for the service of providing the collateral—the painting."

Sergei frowned. "Sounds complicated to me. These must be dangerous deals. What if our customer can't complete the deal or loses some or all of the borrowed money?"

"Sergei, you have watched too many gangster movies. But if a deal goes bad, the lender has a painting that presumably has a value in excess of the loan."

"What if he finds out that the painting is not authentic?"

"The money lender doesn't know who we are. But more likely the deal goes through, we get our cut and the painting back to lend out again."

"But what if the customer says that he got the painting from us?"

"What if? What if? We will use a middleman. No-one will know who we are. Go back to painting. And if someone should come after us, we kill them. Any more questions?"

Boris spoke up. "Francesco, you have described a profitable line of work for us. But next month, at his Paris opening, Marc Libidoux will feature Dilinov and Anton Yevgeny as well as a Giacometti that was thought to be lost, a work by Martiros Saryan that surprisingly," *he looks impish when he says things like that*, thought Sofia as she smiled to herself, "was recently discovered in St. Petersburg—incidentally a particularly brilliant work by Sergei—and several other well-known pre-war artists. Sergei, I know that you have been working hard, but will you be ready?"

Sergei straightened. "Yes. Of course. Alone in Montenegro with my notes, photos, and all those paintings. I have been very productive. The Dilinovs have not been so hard. I have canvasses from the 1930s, brushes, and paints identical to what he used." Sergei scratched his beard. "But the Saryan work is harder. His paintings reflected his emotional state.

I have to try to feel what he felt. In the Tretyakov there is a painting I have studied that he did almost 100 years ago of a street scene in Constantinople. The intense heat, a caravan of camels—you can almost hear the bells around their necks—Muslim women in their veils of black and white slipping silently by. The big dark eyes of the Armenian women. His painting was done in tempura on cardboard. It's rather hard to find or replicate old cardboard."

"So," asked Sofia, "no tempura?"

"No. Oil is better. Saryan did an oil painting that's in the Armenian Painting Gallery in Yerevan; I saw it once and have a photograph of it. The centerpiece is a large tree with fruit on it. There is an abstract animal, not clear what kind—probably a donkey—a woman carrying a bag or basket on her shoulders—again abstract—an old house with a balcony overlooking the street. His Armenian childhood speaks from this painting. It looks like it was painted yesterday—very modern. The French loved his work. He continued to paint until shortly before he died in 1972."

Sofia continued, "You seem to know a lot about him. Is your Saryan like the colorful piece with flowers and a street scene I saw on your easel in Montenegro?"

"Yes. I started working on it in Moscow."

"Why has it taken you so long?" Francesco interrupted. "Can't you work faster?"

"Francesco, this is not a copy," Sergei said indignantly. "I am creating a new painting. Very hard. Sort of a pastiche. Combining elements of several Saryan works makes it harder to detect the fraud, but it runs the risk of being detected by scholars and others who know Saryan's work well. But the problem, Francesco, is not so much in the conception but in the execution. I want this painting to be from the late 1930s. First, I had to find a canvas."

Sofia, fascinated by Sergei's explanation, asked, "And how did you do this?"

"I bought a mediocre—very mediocre—painting from 1932 in Moscow and stripped the canvas down to its sizing. Artists do this a lot to get canvasses that show the surface cracks that some want to give depth to their work. The same can be done with works on paper—particularly when it's hard to get paper that's old enough—although it's delicate work.

"But I'm working on canvas, so I prepared a glue from materials available in the 30s and applied it to the canvas. Once dried the canvas showed the cracks I wanted and it was ready for paint. I used colors and paints that Saryan used. But then the hard part.

"Saryan loved reflected light, and he used a lot of brush drawing. Perhaps he was influenced by old masters or by Poussin or Monet. But I needed fine sable brushes of the kind Saryan used. They are often used for water colors. After much searching, I was able to find satisfactory brushes, and then I went to work. After the glue, then the priming, the under painting, the over painting, glazes, and varnishes.

"It all takes time to dry and to correct. Still harder is making the surface look like it's eighty years old. Oil paint takes many, many years to harden."

Sergei stopped talking and sipped at a glass of wine.

"Sergei," Boris said, "that's more than I have ever heard you talk. You have studied and learned well. But you have us in suspense. How did you solve the hardening of the paint problem?"

"You remember that big oven I had shipped from Belgrade?"

"The truckers thought we were going to use it to make pizza."

"We probably could have. But in studying various techniques necessary to address the question of how to simulate old paint, I noted that some forgers have suggested using heat to stimulate the drying of paint. A famous forger named Van Meegeren described using a fairly primitive oven to bake various layers of paint in creating a fake Vermeer. I recently read that in China there are workshops devoted to producing faked old porcelain and selling it as authentic. These workshops actually build wood-fired kilns, based on the ones that artisans used centuries ago, to harden the glazes. So I decided to use a modern oven capable of achieving high temperatures. My task was not as difficult as that faced by van Meegeren and others who forge old masters. The older the paint is supposed to be, the more difficult it is to get the proper result with the new paint.

"So, I used the oven, and the Saryan, which only has to appear to be about 100 years old, is in Paris as we speak. Here's a photo taken by Libidoux, who is quite excited by the painting."

His three companions rubbed their hands together. "We can't clap or it would attract attention, but that was quite a summary. Your uncle would be proud," said Boris. "Your next project is the Gauguin for our art as collateral business, correct?"

"Yes, I return to the villa tomorrow."

"Good," said Boris. "We need you to keep working. I just heard from Libidoux. He sold the Moscow Picasso to an Asian buyer for the largest amount we have received so far. The buyer got the painting and it checked out so the money is in Libidoux's account in Switzerland. It will be transferred to us in a few days pursuant to our agreement. We will then make the usual distributions."

"My Uncle Andrei has yet to receive anything other than the allowances you have paid us, Boris. He is an old man."

"I know that, Sergei, and funds will be put into Andrei's Moscow accounts as well as yours soon."

"But we don't want to keep all but a small amount of the money in Russia," Sergei said.

"You don't trust the banks of your homeland?" Francesco mocked.

"My uncle has waited a long time for this," said Sergei with some irritation. "Should problems arise, I cannot allow his reward to be put at risk."

Sofia thought: *this is interesting—Sergei looked directly at Francesco, and Francesco looked away. This kid has some toughness in him that I haven't seen.*

"Sergei, shortly, Sofia and I will go to Zurich to visit our money," said Boris. "We will take you and your uncle with us and show you how to keep your money safe from whatever transpires in Russia. Now, go back to work. We are making a lot of money. Let's keep it going."

◆ ◆ ◆

After lunch, Boris and Sofia walked through the labyrinth of narrow streets and canals of Castello to the Church of Santa Maria Formosa, pausing first to look at it across a canal. "An interesting work of architecture," observed Boris, "two façades—in front of us across the canal and one on the campo. But I have brought you here not because of the architecture but to see two paintings." As they entered the church, he pointed out the altar piece. "It's by Palma Vecchio. That's Saint Barbara, and of course Mary cradling the body of Christ. Over there is a marvelous triptych from the fifteenth century by Vivorini."

"Why all the way to look at these pieces?" asked Sofia.

"Because, Sofia, it's important to me and should be important to you to see work that cannot be faked."

On the way back, they stopped by the Church of San Martino to look at Perez's lion.

"It's quite a small lion," observed Sofia.

"But it has a big mouth," Boris laughed.

Chapter Twenty-Two

Paris / Rome

"Assistant Commissioner Terzazo," said Gerard into his phone, "one moment, please. Detective Abou just walked in the room. I will put this call on speaker phone." Gerard pushed the button and continued. "Pierre, I was filling the Assistant Commissioner in on what we learned in Marseilles."

"Good," said Pierre, "I just got some more information."

"Please share it, Detective Abou," said the voice on the speaker.

"As the Senior Inspector has told you, we learned that prior to each murder there was a shipment from Mexico that had docked in Marseilles with a load of refrigerators. We had the port records reviewed and in between those two shipments there was a third from Mexico—this time of microwave ovens. Each of these shipments was loaded onto trucks—trucks that were driven into Italy.

"Well, this morning, one of the dockworkers, reluctantly, but with help from the Marseilles force which had something on him, told our investigator that when each of the trucks were loaded, the process was observed by two or three men who spoke Spanish as well as by several Italians. And the trucks, this fellow said, were driven by Italians."

Terzazo's voice in perfect French came over the speaker. "We have traced the truckloads of refrigerators to Genoa, where they were reloaded on ships. Now we will look for the microwave ovens."

"But why would someone ship refrigerators to Marseilles, truck them to Genoa and reload them onto a ship?" asked Gerard, thinking aloud. "Another detail is that each of these ships was unloaded in the morning. Assistant Commissioner, when did the trucks arrive in Genoa?"

There was silence while paper rustled on the other end of the line.

"It appears that in each case, the trucks arrived in Genoa late in the afternoon of the second day after they left Marseilles."

"Two full days to make a one-day trip. These are very slow trucks," said Pierre.

"Unless they made a stop after they crossed the border into Italy," observed Gerard. "Assistant Commissioner, what is the country like between the French border and Genoa?"

"Hilly, leading to the sea," came the voice from the box. "Many small villages. Small country roads. Plenty of places to pull over and perhaps drive a truck into a garage or barn."

After a few minutes of silence, Gerard said, "Okay, Pierre, what would Sherlock Holmes say about this?"

More silence and then Pierre said, "He once said, I think it was in the *Boscombe Valley Mystery*, something to the effect that 'singularity is almost invariably a clue.' What stands out here is that it took two days to drive the refrigerators from a French port to an Italian port where they were each time reloaded on a ship. Since the refrigerators were the constant, a reasonable conclusion is that the refrigerators contained something that was removed over the course of the two days."

"Assistant Commissioner," said Gerard, "that is my conclusion as well. The contents of the refrigerators were removed probably between the border and Genoa, the refrigerators and ovens now empty of their contents were then trucked to Genoa and shipped out. But that leaves the question as to why the refrigerators were not shipped directly to Genoa if the final destination of the contents was Italy."

"One reason," came Terzazo's reply, "might be that the Genoa port is much smaller than Marseilles, which is of course one of Europe's largest ports. Unloading contraband surreptitiously from the refrigerators in the port area, transporting it out of the port, and then loading the refrigerators onto ships could well be noticed in a smaller port like Genoa. A second reason would be simply to cover their tracks. I'm growing convinced that those refrigerators may have been the packaging for the increased supplies of high-quality heroin and cocaine we have been seeing in Northern Italy."

"But why the Marseilles murders?" said Pierre.

"I'm not sure, but the five in Marseilles may be connected to the two gruesome killings in Naples of lower-level drug dealers that I told you about. Certainly the desecration of the dockworker's bodies points in that direction."

"If the Mexican cartels want to expand their activities into Italy, they would need Italian partners, would they not?"

"Yes, Detective Abou. They would need the locals for their networks of dealers. There are several criminal groups operating in Italy that participate in drug dealing. Some are international in scope. Others are more local. For the smaller players there is a rough geographic division of the business. One group centered around Milan, another in Naples. Both are active in Rome. One of these would be a likely partner."

"So, we may see a partnership emerging between Mexican and Italian criminal elements in Italy," commented Gerard.

"Yes," replied Terzazo, "in the North with perhaps some conflict in the South."

"And with a Marseilles connection as well," said Pierre.

"Well, gentlemen, this has been a very productive meeting," said Terzazo. "I see I have some more work to do."

"As do we, Assistant Commissioner. We now have descriptions of Spanish speaking men—probably Mexicans—who are persons of interest to us in connection with the Marseilles killings. We will keep you informed."

"One question, Senior Inspector, do you still have an international warrant outstanding for Sofia Mostov, the Cuban-Russian woman?"

"Yes we do. You are interested in her as well, are you not?"

"Somewhat. We think she killed a Camorra type on the Amalfi Coast. That's why I'm telling you that one of our cops in Venice, who was looking through photographs of wanted persons, thought he saw someone who looked like her in a café in Venice. Her hair was dark, but from her pictures—she has striking features—he thought he noticed her."

"Interesting," Gerard said. "Please keep us informed."

"The Senior Inspector is particularly interested since she threatened to kill him."

"Pierre is *particularly* interested in my welfare. If something happens to me, he will have to pay for his own lunches."

Terzazo laughed and the call ended.

"Pierre, can you find out if the Marseilles port gets enough notice of incoming ships so that we can organize a surveillance?"

"I will find out. Let's continue this discussion over lunch."

"Okay, but I have promised to take Catherine to lunch. Please join us."

"Gladly, although I detect a change in our lunch-time routine."

Gerard smiled and said he was already late for a senior staff meeting.

"I will see you at lunch. Marie knows to expect three."

Chapter Twenty-Three

Catherine was on the phone when the manager of the Paris office knocked on her door. She motioned him in and pointed to the chair in front of her desk. Once finished, she set the phone down and said, "Victor, I was sent here to help you. And I can't help you without being direct. The customer we met with yesterday is the CEO of one of the largest primary insurance carriers in Belgium. He wants to know what our conclusions are on the Brussels boiler explosion."

"I told him—it was an accident."

"Victor, L & M gets paid a significant amount of money to investigate claims, not just recommend that they get paid. Since I was only part way into my review of the file when you gave me two hours' notice of the lunch, I sat there while you went over the obvious facts. I said little because I didn't want intra-office friction to come through to a customer.

"Now let me tell you what may have happened. The boiler exploded even though the system provided for both a visible and audible alarm in the system when the pressure got to a dangerous point. The system was checked three weeks before the explosion and was certified as working fine. Our client employed an outside firm to manage security in the factory including monitoring of critical systems. According to the contract with the security firm, which is in our file but apparently had not been reviewed carefully by anyone in this office, an employee of the security firm is supposed to be in the control room 24-7.

"If there was a security firm employee in the control room, why didn't he or she respond to the alarm? I asked Albert, who you kindly assigned to assist me, to do some research. In that system, the interval between an alarm being sounded and the pressure building up to the point of an explosion is twenty minutes. So either the security firm employee had left their post or was asleep—very much asleep—given the noise the alarm supposedly makes. I asked Albert to call our client in Brussels and ask if they keep personnel records on the employees of the security firm. Not surprisingly, they don't.

"Our next step will be to see if we can access such records directly from the security firm. Not likely without some kind of legal process. Also, no one from this office interviewed any employee of the security firm. We depended on the report of the Brussels police. Pretty sketchy. Nor have we done any probing into the financial situation of our client. All there is in the file is a two-year old audit by a small Belgian accounting firm. No supporting documentation. Not even credit reports."

Catherine paused to drink coffee from a cup on her desk. The office manager, his face flushed, didn't see her wince. "Madam York, we have just begun our investigation. I'm sure we would have the facts you just related."

Catherine sat silently and looked at Victor. She had described him to Gerard as a well-tailored yes-man. She took a paper from the file on her desk, and said, "Victor, you have recommended that the claim be paid with no further action. Our job is not just to shuffle some paper and then pay a claim, it's to investigate a claim. In this situation it's possible that our client caused this loss in order to get the insurance proceeds or, more likely at this point, that the security firm was negligent, in which case we have a subrogation claim against them on behalf of our client. We will continue this discussion later.

I will personally direct the next stage of this investigation."

As a visibly shaken Victor backed out of her office, Catherine asked, "Have you ever been to an art gallery called Galerie Libidoux over on the Avenue Matignon?"

"I have walked past it, but I have never been in it. Why?"

"A Swiss primary coverage insurer that we work with is providing coverage to the gallery and the New York office is taking a piece. It seems a bit unusual because the Libidoux gallery is representing a Swiss company owned by a Russian who has a large art collection that is being sold in part through this Paris gallery. Libidoux is apparently responsible for insuring a number of the pieces—some of which he, the Russian collector, and a Mexican, who also has a gallery in Venice, jointly own. We also provide some coverage to the same Mexican who has a large art collection in Mexico City."

"Is it legitimate?" Victor asked.

"Legal in New York says this art dealer has an insurable interest. And we are just taking the last layer of coverage. But my career at L & M, as you know, has been mostly in claims investigations, and my experience is that the more complex the ownership of an asset, the more difficult the investigation."

"But there are no claims on the art, are there?" the manager asked anxiously.

"No. And let's hope it stays that way."

◆　◆　◆

That night Catherine and Gerard, along with a banker friend of Gerard and his wife, had dinner at a restaurant on the Avenue Kléber, known for its seafood. As they walked back to the Île Saint-Louis, Catherine commented on her first course. "I have never had a carpaccio of beet roots and marinated tuna. What a delightful combination, and it went well with the snapper."

"Yes, flavoring the fish with a puree of chervil was a nice

touch. But I prefer my fish prepared simply. There seems to be enough complexity in my work life now for me."

"You seemed quiet tonight. Why?"

"We are working on a case in Marseilles and in Italy that may involve substantial drug smuggling into Italy, and I worry that the activity could spread here as well."

"Interesting, I am seeing more complications in the underwritings that come through our Paris office. We are looking at coverage for art owned by a Russian through a Swiss holding company, being sold by a Paris art dealer, along with a Mexican who has a gallery in Venice."

"Do you know who the Mexican is?"

"Francesco Perez. Why do you ask?"

"Oh, only because the drugs in this case may originate in Mexico. Seems to me unusual for a Mexican to own an art gallery in Venice."

"It's a global economy, Gerard," Catherine smiled.

Gerard laughed. "It is, indeed. But enough business talk. Let me take your hand and enjoy with you the moon reflecting off the Seine."

Chapter Twenty-Four

Sitting in Marc Libidoux's conference room, Libidoux, Francesco Perez, and Boris Voroshilov were poring over a list of paintings and occasionally walking over to look at several propped up against the wall.

"Marc, do you think we should approach Sidney Pebbles and do a private treaty arrangement for one or two of our pieces? The Monet and the Picasso are both well-known works, and the provenance issue would complicate putting them in an auction, as we have seen. And we have a special interest in keeping out of the spotlight."

"Boris, there is a risk that Madame Letto at Pebbles might do her cop routine and advise Pebbles against such a deal."

"Marc, you worry too much. There are buyers out there who want a Monet or a Picasso so badly they would pull the trigger themselves. We make it clear to Pebbles that Madame Letto is to be ignored."

When Perez was finished talking the room fell silent. Then, Libidoux said, "It's worth an inquiry. The private treaty approach keeps the transaction confidential. An auction is public even if the name of the consignor and successful bidder is not; the private treaty sale as well as the identity of both parties is private and the transaction more likely to remain confidential. We could stimulate interest in the collection of the anonymous Russian by opening negotiations with the auction house. I could stoke the fire by suggesting a higher price than the auction house wants to sell the piece for.

"I told Pebbles that we had a Picasso and a Chagall that we might consign to him for his fall auction, but that we would want a guarantee."

"What did he say?"

"That he was just starting his business, and that he would put a maximum on any guarantee."

"Well, he could bring in an outside guarantor and pay him a commission to hedge his risk."

"And," said Perez, "perhaps I could create the impression of how valuable our work is by using one of our entities to provide the guarantee. The auction house wouldn't know of the connection. Besides, we could whet Pebble's appetite by raising the potential of a big profit by agreeing to a conservative price for his guarantee. If the painting sells above the guarantee, we would pay him a fee for that, he would get the buyer's premium, and my colleagues would get a fee for the guarantee."

"We should do some private treaty deals," said Libidoux. "But for now, the priority is to sell a lot of works at my show that opens in two weeks.

"After that we can look at private treaties and continue to sell into the Asian and Gulf market. Sergei's early de Kooning is an excellent job. I can sell it to a Singapore buyer. Maybe we sell the original later—to a collector from the United Arab Emirates I know. Both of these guys keep their collections private so neither is likely to discover the other."

"So," commented Boris, "your show will feature seven of Sergei's Dilinovs, two of his Yevgenys, his Saryan, one of his Klees, and six to eight of the paintings from Moscow. Is that enough?"

"Boris, while I would like more works, I think that's enough, and the quality will be so high that we'll get a lot of attention. This anonymous Russian is going to be seen as a big-time collector."

"Marc, you are handling security and insurance?"

"Of course. Who knows—if sales of the Dilinovs and the Yevgenys are slow, maybe there will be a theft."

Chapter Twenty-Five

"Well, Sofia, is this restaurant out of the way enough for you?"

"Yes, Francesco, thank you for choosing it. I'm confident that my altered appearance will fool the police, but there is an international warrant out for me, and the French police seem to have a special interest, so not calling attention to myself seems prudent."

"But you will miss Libidoux's big opening in a few days."

"Exactly the kind of public place that Boris and I should avoid."

Francesco looked at her for a long time and then as if he had kept his feelings bottled up, they now emerged without even a preamble. "I want to talk to you about us. You are a beautiful and strong woman. I am fascinated by you. I would like to spend time with you. I can protect you—here and in Italy. We can travel in Mexico, spend time in your beloved Cuba, go to South America, Russia—wherever you want to travel. I am very rich. You won't have to be concerned about these complex schemes to get money. I will take care of you." And he reached across the table to put his hands over Sofia's.

As she gently, but firmly, removed her hands from his, she said, "Francesco, you are an attractive man. I like men. But understand something about me. My father was a Russian. He was a KGB agent stationed in Cuba. My mother was Cuban. When I was twelve, Boris called my mother from Moscow to tell her that my father had been killed in a KGB operation. My mother screamed and cried for three days. She had no one, no relative. Because of my father's work and my mother's lack of interest, we had no friends in Cuba. She hardly talked to me when I was growing up. He was her life—her whole life.

"A month later, some neighbors came to the door with a police officer to tell me that my mother had drowned. No other information. A hug. Some food. They left. I sat in that apartment alone for two days and two nights. I couldn't cry. I couldn't leave. I will never forget that feeling. It was as if I was suspended in a place with no air, no light, nothingness. Helpless. Abandoned.

"Then my Uncle Boris called me from Moscow. He told me I was coming to Moscow to live with him. A woman from the Russian Embassy came to the apartment, brought me dinner, helped me pack, stayed with me that night, and took me to the airport the next day.

"I had never been on a plane before. Not only was I scared, I was going to a place I didn't know. My father taught me to speak Russian, but I didn't know Russia—only Cuba.

"I felt helpless and alone on that trip. I had no money—not one ruble." She looked away.

After a long moment, Perez thought, *she's in another place. I must bring her back.* "So you lived with Boris and became an operative like your father and uncle."

"Yes, my uncle rescued me from the Soviet athletic machine. They were grooming me for the shot put and discus. The KGB training was hard. I was young and there were few women operatives. But I was determined and tough. The organization became my family. But, Francesco, one thought that never left me was that my mother was weak. My father was her life. I decided during those years that I would never be dependent on a man, and I would never be poor—no matter what it would take to get rich. I trained hard, and I did

whatever the organization asked of me. Then, with their bless-
ing, I left the organization, although I continue to be an asset
for them. A lot of rich Russians come to St. Barth. And some
get into trouble and most talk too much. I started a jewelry
business—and for the first time in my life I had money. I
loved the independence that wealth gave me. I want both.

"So, you can see that I am not the woman for you. Our arrangement for now is and must be one of business. But when
this art operation is finished...." She didn't complete the sentence.

"Sofia, I hear what you are saying, but in this romantic
Mexican heart there is still a hope that you will change your
mind. One thing you might consider is what if I gave you the
Venice gallery. You understand art, and you're very effective
at selling expensive items to rich people—particularly men."

Sofia smiled slightly. Perez thought she hardly ever smiled.
"I am finished with retail—no matter how high-end. But you
are very generous. Your offer means a lot to me. Besides, do
you have enough to keep you busy in Italy without the gallery?"

"The gallery was something I always wanted to try, but it
will become a burden. It's a means to the end of capitalizing
on the art find your Russian friends discovered. There is much
more money to be made and over a longer period of time by
expanding the drug business in Italy and beyond."

"You have talked very little about that."

"I trust you, so I will tell you my plan. It can make me and
my colleagues much money." He paused and looked at her,
"And there is always room for another partner who is willing
to do whatever is asked of her." He then went on to describe
how he and an Italian group were distributing drugs in Italy,
saying that, "Italy is fertile ground for expanding our business. The Italians in this business are complacent. They divide
up the country between north and south and are content.
Maybe there is a bit of friction over the middle, but basically

they are satisfied with their arrangements with each other and with the politicians and the police, whose major concern is keeping the violence under control.

"But their model is old-fashioned. It's not global in concept. They don't much care to grow. They are satisfied with what they have. Maybe it's their beautiful country. I don't know, but that's not how we will approach the business in Italy. We will continually expand our reach, first in Italy and then beyond. And if we don't seize the opportunity to be aggressive in Italy, the Russians will. While these paintings are very profitable today, the real money here is in white powder, not paint."

Perez continued to talk as they finished their meal, and the couple decided to leave the restaurant separately. After Perez left, Sofia reached into her purse and turned off a small voice recorder. She then poured herself another glass of wine.

Chapter Twenty-Six

PARIS

As they got into Gerard's BMW in the parking garage near his building, Gerard commented on how beautiful Catherine looked. Her short black dress, fitted at the hem and at the waist was accented by a thin diamond necklace. "Are those new shoes?"

"Yes, an old dress and Christian Louboutin shoes that I bought today. How long I can stand on these heels I don't know, but I love the trim on the straps and the red soles. They did cost as much as my bonus!"

"Very elegant. Not the typical uniform of an insurance executive. But then again you are hardly typical." He leaned over and kissed her. "Explain again why we are going."

"It's business, Gerard. The New York office has agreed to participate in the coverage for a new customer in Paris. An art dealer named Marc Libidoux. It's a questionable underwriting. There's an opening tonight in his gallery on the Avenue Matignon. The ownership of the works he's showing is a bit murky for my suspicious mind."

"Well, then, we'd better not be late," Gerard said, before removing a red light from the center console and putting it on the dashboard.

"Gerard, that flashing red light must impress the ladies."

"It helps with the Paris traffic and parking—and I reserve this car for only the most beautiful of women."

As they entered Gallery Libidoux, Gerard said, "At these openings the guests drink lukewarm champagne and once in a while look at the art."

Catherine put her arm through his and said, "Okay, Mr. Stuffy Policeman, enjoy the evening. We won't stay long."

The Gallery Libidoux was already crowded. Paintings covered the walls of the two exhibition spaces. Elegantly dressed men and women greeted each other and drank champagne being served by two slim young women wearing short black dresses. Others stood in Libidoux's conference room, which had been converted into a bar for the evening. Libidoux's assistant circulated through the crowd, discretely telling people that a price list was available in the office.

Catherine found the work of Ilia Dilinov interesting. The bright colors, the brushwork, the abstraction blended with images of what could be urban scenes all demonstrated a serious talent. The works were dated, 1939, 1940, and 1941. The commentary on the wall described him as a young Russian artist who worked in Paris in the late 1930s, then returned to Russia to serve in the Red Army. He continued to paint while in the army and then died in the battle of Stalingrad. One of his paintings was part of the permanent collection of the Musee d'Orsay, another was owned by the Museum of Modern Art in New York, and several were in private collections and museums in Russia.

Another person she noticed studying the Dilinov paintings was a very short and stooped old man with a grey beard wearing a well-worn tweed suit that seemed out of place among the well-dressed crowd. He looked at each Dilinov for a long time, shaking his head and muttering to himself.

Standing in a corner of the first exhibition room, Sofia Mostov was talking to Libidoux. Her hair was a dark brown, she was dressed in a non-descript pair of slacks and a shapeless sweater. She wore glasses with thick frames.

"Marc, you have to be pleased with the turnout."

"I am, we have already sold a Yevgeny."

"I see your assistant putting a red dot on the Yevgeny next to the door. Do you know the woman standing near it?"

"The attractive brunette talking to the tall grey-haired guy?"

"Yes."

"She's with the insurance company providing coverage on these paintings. She gave me her card just a few minutes ago. Here it is."

Sofia didn't need to look.

"Do you know her?" said Libidoux, noticing Sofia closely watching the woman.

"Oh yes. I know her. She's the last person I expected to see in Paris. And here of all places. Do you know the man she was talking to, the one walking into the other room?"

Libidoux looked. "No."

"Well, I'll tell you who he is. He's a big shot French detective. This is too much. I have to leave. Is there a back door out of here?"

"There's a door next to my office. It leads to stairs that will take you to the street. But if you leave, you'll miss Perez. He will be disappointed."

"Greet him for me."

Catherine was studying a beautiful Cezanne painting that was listed on Libidoux's coverage application when she noticed a dark haired woman in glasses walk toward the Gallery office. Something isn't right she thought. Her memory went back to a beach in St. Barth. It was as if the baggy sweater was covering up a shapely figure. She looked at the woman more closely. The woman then turned to look at her. *It can't be! I think this woman is Sofia Mostov! She felt her heart pounding. What would Sofia Mostov be doing in Paris? And why the dark hair, the stooped posture and the awful sweater? It is her. I'm sure. She has disguised herself. She's leaving. Where is Gerard? What if she gets away? I had better follow her. I can call Gerard on my phone.*

Catherine followed Sofia through the door and found herself next to a flight of stairs. The space was dimly lit. The walls concrete. The stairs led down to a landing where they made an abrupt left angle. As Catherine started down the stairs, out of the shadows stepped Sofia Mostov. She was pointing a small pistol at Catherine.

"*Bon soir*, Catherine York. I never thought that I would see you again. Don't move, and put your bag on the floor. Why are you following me?"

Catherine opened her mouth to reply, but she was too startled to even talk.

"So, you are an insurance investigator. And you were in St. Barth to investigate me. And the investment company executive was just a cover. Am I not correct? Well done. What did you find out about me?"

"That you had some wonderful jewelry in your store."

"You are not in a position to make jokes. I see that the French detective who came to St. Barth and tried to arrest me is here too. I don't believe in coincidences. Are the two of you working together? Or perhaps a couple. How romantic. Does he know that I am in Paris?"

Catherine didn't respond.

"You aren't very talkative, but you are a problem for me. If the detective doesn't know that I'm here, you will tell him. And I'm sure he would be delighted to arrest me. Following me was a bad idea."

Catherine nervously shifted.

"Stand still! It would be an even worse idea if you tried anything."

The door to the gallery opened, and the two women both turned to look up. Gerard stood at the top of the stairs. A deafening shot rang out next to Catherine's ear as Sofia fired at Gerard. The sound echoed off the concrete walls and stairs.

"Catherine, get down!" shouted Gerard as he fired at Sofia, who grabbed Catherine and held her as a shield.

"Drop your gun and kick it down the stairs de Rochenoir or I will kill this woman."

As Sofia pointed her gun at Gerard, Catherine freed herself from Sofia's grasp and jammed her elbow in Sofia's side. Grabbing at the neck of Catherine's dress with one hand, Sofia got off another shot at Gerard, but it went wide as Sofia punched her arm as she fired. As the women struggled on the landing, Sofia pulled Catherine toward the stairs, and one of Catherine's slim high heels caught in the grating of the stair. Her ankle twisted and she tumbled down headfirst. Sofia bolted down the remaining stairs and out the door to the Rue St. Honorée.

Gerard called for assistance on his cell phone as he ran down to Catherine and helped her up. "Are you ok?"

Catherine sat on one the stairs and rubbed her bleeding elbow. "I'm fine. Go after Sofia, but be careful."

Holding his police identification in one hand and his Sig Sauer in the other, Gerard cautiously opened the door to the street. A policewoman who had been standing close by as part of the heavy security presence in that part of Paris came running to him as a police car with sirens blaring pulled up.

"Did you see a woman coming out of this door a few moments ago?"

"Oui, Oui," said the officer, "and I heard shots from inside this building. Is anyone hurt?"

"There is a woman on the stairs inside. She isn't shot but she's injured. Please call an ambulance and go in and assist her. The woman who came out of the door—which way did she go?"

Pointing to the right, she said, "She turned and walked up the Avenue Matignon."

Jumping into the backseat of the police car, Gerard

LAWRENCE PERLMAN | 158

instructed the driver to make a U turn and head up the Avenue Matignon, in the direction away from the Champs Elysee. Meanwhile, Sofia having thrown her black wig into a trash can, ran into the street where a car had stopped to let a police car pass. Pointing her gun at the startled driver, she ordered him out, and as he left the car she hit him on the side of his head with her gun. He fell to the street. Saying to herself, *that should keep them occupied for a while,* she drove a few hundred yards and turned east onto the rue de Penthiere, taking it to the Boulevard Malsherbes and then to the busy St. Lazare railroad station where she parked in an underground ramp. Avoiding the Metro with its surveillance cameras, she took three buses to the small hotel in an obscure part of north Paris where she could spend the night before moving on.

Francisco Perez walked into the Gallery and over to Libidoux and said, "What is going on, I just heard gun shots."

"Are you sure?" asked Libidoux.

"You are damned right I am sure. And where is Sofia? I don't see her here."

"I don't know. She saw some people that she didn't want to see. One was a cop. And I think she left. Maybe through the door next to my office."

Hurrying to the door, Perez opened it and saw an officer standing over a woman sitting on the stairs. The policewoman shouted at him, "Get away from here. This is a crime scene." Perez wasn't sure who the woman on the stairs was, but seeing that it wasn't Sofia, he went back into the gallery, which was emptying quickly. Encountering Libidoux, who was sweating profusely, he said, "I don't know what's going on. Now I hear sirens. I'm getting out of here."

◆ ◆ ◆

Later that evening, Catherine was still up when Gerard entered the Ile St. Louis apartment. He hugged her and said, "How are you feeling?"

"A sprained ankle and a bruised elbow. Nothing too serious. Did you get her?"

"No. She's one of the most elusive criminals I've encountered."

"Dammit!"

"My feelings exactly."

"The next time I tangle with a criminal, I won't be wearing high heels."

"No more next times, Catherine my love. You were brave to follow Sofia, but she is very dangerous, particularly when she feels cornered. Let the police deal with her. But thank you for hitting her arm when she was shooting at me. She's a very good shot."

"Do you really think she would have killed me?"

"You seem remarkably calm about the prospect," said Gerard.

"I was so worried about you. I think I held everything back until I knew that you were safe. Maybe I suspended my reaction. I don't know. The doctor who treated me gave me a sedative. But now what happened is hitting me."

"You're shaking. Let me hold you." Gerard kissed her through her tears.

As they sat on a sofa holding each other, Gerard said, "I don't know what she would have done. By the time you encountered her, she had no reason to kill you except perhaps some warped idea of a payback. I saw her so she was aware that I knew she was in Paris. We certainly don't need your testimony to convict her of insurance fraud. But she's a trained assassin, and she may have decided on the spot to get rid of you, perhaps me as well. If she sees us as a threat, she's trained to eliminate us. Her training was designed to put her almost on auto-pilot if she decides that her mission is to kill us. I'm going to assign someone to protect you when you're not with me and someone else to watch this building. Perhaps you should take a day off from the office."

"Thank you. But now that I've stopped shaking, I'll be fine. I can get around okay on this ankle. But how will I explain a bodyguard to the folks at the office?"

"She will be unobtrusive. But, my dear, I'm sure you'll think of something." He kissed her forehead.

Chapter Twenty-Seven

FLORENCE

In the Oltrarno neighborhood of Florence, near the Ponte Vecchio there is a plain-looking church called Santa Felicita. Ettore Grassi entered and immediately turned toward the small chapel to his right. Sitting inside was a slim and elegantly dressed man in his mid-forties. Grassi sat down next to him. Staring up at the frescoes by the artist, Jacopo Pontormo, Grassi thought how much his father would be moved by the paintings and the vibrant and beautiful colors the artist used to give power to his deeply religious themes.

"I would come to Florence just to experience this place," the man next to him said. "To think that a sixteenth-century artist could use pinks and blues this way."

"A good place for two art lovers to meet when neither Rome nor Milan would be a wise choice," Grassi responded. Neither man looked at the other. "How is your family, Steffani?"

"All healthy—and your father?"

"Also healthy. I would like to bring him to this church, but these days he doesn't want to leave Venice."

"Please give him my regards." Terzazo's tone changed. "Have you been to Naples recently?"

"No, why do you ask?" Grassi said, still looking up at the Pontormo frescoes.

"I understand there is some unhappiness there with a newly aggressive player who is upsetting the established order."

"There are often newcomers who see our fields as holding a potentially rich harvest."

"Yes, of course, and they never seem to fit into our old way of doing things. I'm sure you know about the two killings in Naples."

"Yes—the beheadings—gruesome."

"Gruesome, indeed. Let me tell you what I know about some shootings in Marseilles."

Terzazo turned to Grassi and talked very quietly for several minutes. Grassi put his left hand on his forehead and gesturing with his right hand, he responded. Terzazo nodded and Grassi got up, crossed himself, and walked into the bright Florentine sunshine.

♦ ♦ ♦

Leaning across the table in the small, dark restaurant, the elder Grassi leaned over close to his son and said, "Thank you for taking me to Paris. It was a good trip. But I find it harder and harder to leave Venice. Even to leave for Florence. You were there yesterday, and you saw the Pontormos?"

"*Si*, Padre. They are breathtaking."

"How can one use the same term—painting—to describe the frescoes of Santa Felicita and the work being shown by your Mexican friend?"

"A friend he is not. The Assistant Director made it clear that the aggressive tactics of the Mexicans are not acceptable," and he went on to summarize the conversation in the Florence church.

"Well, you tried to improve the profitability of our distribution network with more and higher-quality product. But, *non tutte le ciambelle riescono col buco.*"

Ettore smiled and said, "Indeed, not all doughnuts come out with holes. And a smart baker doesn't continue to try to make good pastry out of bad dough."

His father nodded, patted Ettore on the shoulder and said, "You know what to do my son," and resumed looking out over the water at San Giorgio Maggiore.

Chapter Twenty-Eight

"What's on your mind, Libidoux, that was so important that I come here?" Sofia said, as she took a seat in his office.

"I didn't want to talk on the phone, but we may have a problem. Yesterday, I was visited by a man who identified himself as Laurent Gallet. Here is his card." And he pushed it across his desk to Sofia with one finger as if he wanted to touch it as little as possible.

"He is an art consultant. So what?"

"He claims to be an expert on Dilinov. He wanted to tell me that he doesn't think the Dilinovs in my show are authentic."

Sofia sat silently. Then she said, "What are his credentials?"

"I have checked him out. His specialty is Russian modernist art. He has written several articles about Dilinov, and he has been consulted by collectors and museums here in Paris as well as other places. He's credible."

"What does he want?"

"He wants me to remove the Dilinovs from the show. I told him that would be impossible. That these were works from a Russian collector who is completely satisfied with their authenticity. He wanted to know who the collector was, and I told him that his identity was confidential."

"What is he like?"

"He's old and eccentric. Probably in his eighties. I noticed him at the opening; he was staring at the Dilinovs and mumbling to himself. He said to me that he would bring his suspicions to the police. We have sold three Dilinovs, each in excess of two million Euros. Even a soupçon of doubt could sink those transactions and raise doubts about me."

"Can we buy him off?"

"I don't think so. He's an old man. His whole persona is wrapped up in his expertise—and above all, his knowledge of Dilinov. He also said he had questions about our Yevgenys."

"I will take his card and talk to Boris."

"I don't think we have much time. He was agitated when he left. He was quite serious about the police and, strange as he is, he may well have enough credibility to get the art police involved."

"We can't let that happen."

Chapter Twenty-Nine

A bored French policeman sat in his office facing a nervous, grey-haired man whom he estimated to be in his mid- to late eighties. Looking at his computer screen, the policeman said, "Monsieur Gallet, I see that we have consulted with you before. I understand that you're concerned about the authenticity of some paintings."

"They're fakes!"

"How can you be so sure?"

"I know."

"But how do you know?"

"I have studied this artist—the Russian Dilinov—I know his work intimately. Perhaps one of the paintings at this Gallery Libidoux would not have concerned me, but looking at a group, they are not right. All done with similar brush strokes, all with bright colors and the light. He wouldn't have painted so many works in such a similar palette and feel. And the works from 1940 and 1941. He was in the Red Army. He painted while he was in the army. He saw terrible things. He was at the siege of Stalingrad. His work from that time wasn't done with bright colors and with sunshine." He stopped to take a breath, and the police officer poured a glass of water for him.

After a pause and wiping his forehead with a handkerchief, Gallet went on, "His work when he went back to Russia at the end of 1939 became increasingly dark. He used greys and blacks. One painting now in a Moscow museum is all in grey, black, and white with a powerful red slash across it. He called it "Blood." He painted it in 1941. There is a Dilinov painting this Libidoux has with a 1941 date that's all bright colors. Not right."

"Have you talked to the gallerist?"

"Yes, yes. A Marc Libidoux. He doesn't want to hear. Says that the paintings came from an anonymous Russian collector, that they are authentic, that they were first shown last month in Venice and nobody raised any questions."

"Did he say how this Russian collector came by the work?"

"Only that he acquired most of them from possessions of Dilinov's family—all of whom perished in the war. Others came from French and German dealers after the war."

"That is plausible. German dealers who had aided the Nazis in their plunders became legitimate—in their eyes—after the war. Some even sold works to museums that had previously owned them. And here in France, as well as in Germany, there was a black market in art along with a lot of questionable authentications."

"I heard some of that from Monsieur Libidoux," said Gallet. "While some of the stolen art ended up in Western Germany, much stayed in East Germany and found its way back to the Soviet Union. As if it makes any difference to the matter of fakes. Libidoux said that provenance started new after the Soviets issued an order that any art stolen by the Nazis would be confiscated and become the property of the Soviet Union."

"Well, that's right. We don't accept that the Soviet order applies in the West, but it's a murky area when ownership of a piece is challenged."

Gallet stood up and clenched his fist. He almost screamed, "This is not about ownership! It's about faking the work of a great and underestimated artist! The work is for sale. To sell a forgery is a crime."

"Please, Mr. Gallet, sit down. As of now, it would be your word against that of dealers in Paris and Venice and whoever would represent the owner. We can talk to this Libidoux, who is becoming prominent in the Paris art scene, but to do anything more, we need more. We need evidence."

Still standing, Gallet said, "My eye is all the evidence you need. But I am meeting someone this evening who says that she can give me more information. Inspector, you haven't seen the last of me." And he stormed out of the office.

Chapter Thirty

MARSEILLES

"Welcome to North Africa in France," said Inspector Maurice Monsey of the Marseilles police force as Gerard and Pierre entered the small room at the back of the restaurant on the Rue du Musée. The street was crowded with men, some wearing robes and some western clothes, women in kaftans, as well as a sprinkling of tourists gawking at the street vendors and hookah cafes lining the street.

Monsey was sitting with three other men, all wearing civilian clothes. He rose to shake hands with the two Parisian policemen and said, "I thought this was an inconspicuous place for us to meet, and that you might enjoy the North African food that many of the restaurants in this neighborhood do so well. I have taken the liberty of ordering lamb, sausages, and chicken to put on the couscous. We seldom have the honor of welcoming here such a distinguished policeman as you, Senior Inspector de Rochenoir, and of course we are always pleased to see our native son, Detective Abou. Let me introduce my fellow officers."

Gerard responded, "The news that a ship from Mexico is arriving in Marseilles with a load of refrigerators among its cargo certainly got our interest, and thank you for hosting this dinner."

At that point, heaping platters of couscous, meats, and vegetables were brought into the room. Conversation turned to the food until the waiters had left and closed the door.

Pierre looked at the closed door, and Monsey said, "Don't worry, our conversation is secure here, and I have two men in the main restaurant as well."

Gerard said, "Inspector Monsey, please describe your plan."

"We know the pier the ship will be docking at. It's expected to arrive tomorrow about eight-thirty in the morning. The routine in the port is that after a ship has docked the containers are unloaded from the ship and then moved to several locations where they are opened and inspected by customs officials. Once cleared, the contents are either loaded on trucks or put back into the containers for shipment by train.

"We expect two trucks from Italy to arrive at the port early in the morning. Thank you for arranging with the border police to alert us when the trucks enter France." Gerard nodded his head. "The container with the refrigerators will be moved to a location that we'll have under surveillance. We'll go over a map of the port with you tomorrow morning. The crated refrigerators will be unloaded—and the customs inspector, who we're certain has been bribed, will open one or two crates, perhaps a refrigerator, sign some forms, and leave. Dockworkers will then use fork lifts to move the crates into the trucks.

"Based on what we learned in investigating the shootings of the dockworkers last month, there will probably be between two and four Mexicans observing the process as well as several Italians. The truck drivers will be Italians.

"We'll have fifteen police concealed in the immediate area and others at the perimeter of the port. When the customs inspector leaves, we'll arrest him out of sight and then we'll show ourselves, with weapons drawn, detain the Italians and Mexicans, if they are there, and search the refrigerators. If we find what we think we'll find, I'll call for patrol wagons. The perps will be loaded into them and taken to headquarters, the trucks impounded, and the site guarded until our trucks can move the evidence."

"A good plan," Gerard said. "Let me fill you in on another element of this." He then proceeded to describe the conversations between the Italian and French police.

"So, you want to invite the Italians to witness the bust?"

"No. No. The fewer people who know the more likely that we'll be successful. I will inform my Italian counterpart after we've apprehended the criminals; he may want to participate in their interrogations. I'm sure it would be his preference if we allowed the transfer to take place and followed the trucks into Italy, where the Italian police could observe the transfer of the merchandise, but that would introduce too many variables. In an operation like this, the fewer the variables the higher the likelihood of success."

The group continued to discuss the planning and agreed to meet early tomorrow morning at Marseilles police headquarters.

◆ ◆ ◆

As the morning sun rose into a cloudless sky over the sparkling Mediterranean, police vans and cars entered the sprawling Marseilles port from several directions and parked inside two buildings near an unloading shed where the containers from the Mexican freighter had been scheduled to be unloaded. The freighter itself was at that moment being guided to its berth.

The Marseilles police had set up a command post in one of the buildings, and Maurice Monsey, several of his assistants, Pierre, and Gerard were clustered around a makeshift table. Gerard and Pierre studied the diagram of the port while Monsey was on the radio confirming that his police were in position. A female officer wearing a protective vest checked the action on her automatic weapon as Pierre loaded two magazines for his Sig Sauer S.P. pistol. He whispered to Gerard that he had never seen Monsey so organized and professional.

"He is obviously trying to impress you."

"If my presence motivates him, all the better."

Two hours and several cups of coffee later, Monsey reported that the ship was being unloaded, and that the refrigerator container was the first to come off.

Then he said that one of his officers had just radioed that two trucks and two cars with Italian license plates had cleared port security and were headed to the unloading area. Pierre and the female officer were posted at a window. They signaled that the trucks had arrived.

Then Monsey said into his radio, "How many?" He turned to Gerard and Pierre and said, "The Mexicans have arrived and, they're walking toward the unloading area."

The detectives watched as the containers from the ship were hauled to the shed in front of them on small flatbed trucks. The two Italian trucks drove close by and parked. Forklifts were driven up, and the dockworkers proceeded to unload crates from the containers. A single customs inspector stood by. The dockworkers opened two crates, and the customs inspector undid the strapping around two of the refrigerators in each crate, opened the refrigerator doors, and peered inside.

Looking through her binoculars, the police officer said, "The customs guy is talking to one of the Italians. The inspector just signed and stamped a paper on his clipboard. It looks like he's giving a paper to the Italian. Their backs are to me, but I think the Italian just gave the customs inspector an envelope."

"Good," said Monsey. "My men will stop him as soon as he rounds the corner of that grey building. Then we'll move in." Pushing his earpiece more tightly into his ear, Monsey said, "Okay, he's being stopped. Let's go." He then stepped out of the command post building with a megaphone, wearing a protective vest over his uniform. He was accompanied by four uniformed officers, all wearing protective vests and carrying FAMAS assault rifles.

"This is a police operation," a voice boomed. "You are all

under arrest. Face the grey wall behind you with your hands raised. Do not resist or you will be shot."

As the four truck drivers raised their hands and walked to the wall of the shed, the police told the dockworkers to leave. Taking advantage of the cover provided by the departing dock workers and the truck drivers moving to the wall, the remaining four Italians ran around the corner of the shed. Monsey directed the four policeman to go after them, while he directed two others to move around the other side of the shed to cut them off. As the police officers carefully moved around the corner of the shed, shots rang out, and the police returned the fire with their FAMAS rifles. The Italians ran toward one of their cars, continuing to fire with their Beretta pistols. They managed to get the driver's door of one of the cars open before it was riddled by 5.62 mm NATO rounds from the FAMAS rifles. One of the Italians went down, and the three others raised their hands and dropped their weapons as more French police came up behind them.

Several other officers, along with Pierre, ran out of the command post towards where the Mexicans had been spotted. The Mexicans shot at the pursuing police from behind a crane. Pierre and the officers took cover behind a stack of shipping containers. The policewoman used her automatic weapon to provide covering fire, as Pierre and two officers ran to a shed that cut off the escape route toward the gate to the port.

"She's dropped one of them. The others are moving toward that storage shed. Let's go after them," shouted Pierre.

A police vehicle appeared and the Mexicans fired on it. The gunman then turned and fired at Pierre and the two Marseilles cops with him. Pierre motioned for the two officers to go around one side of the shed while he went around the other side. Another police car stopped in front of a running Mexican and crouching behind an opened car door, the officer shouted, "Stop and drop your weapon."

Weapons drawn, several officers followed Pierre around the shed as another shot was fired at them. The Mexicans seemed to be using their weapons to distract the police as the Italians ran through the port. One Italian was stopped by the policewoman with the automatic weapon, another tackled by a burly Marseilles cop as he tried to run.

The Mexicans ran toward the hill leading out of the port as police sirens blared. One fired on a pursuing police vehicle, the bullet shattering its rear window.

The police officer and the Mexican exchanged shots, and the Mexican went down. Another one climbed on a forklift, started it, raised the two lethal forks, and began driving it toward Pierre. Pierre fired three shots at the rapidly approaching forklift. The driver fell off, clutching his shoulder. The forklift swerved into the shed, its two forks smashing the door. Pierre ran up to the shooter, kicked his gun away, and rolled him on his stomach. Then he handcuffed him.

Just then he heard a shot. He turned to see another Mexican on the ground. Gerard standing over him, his gun in his hand.

"Thank you, Gerard, I didn't see him."

"You're too good a partner for me to let him shoot you. It's bad enough that the guy you shot tried to impale you on a forklift." Gerard then spoke into his radio. "We have apprehended the eight Italians and four Mexicans. No injuries on our side except for a sprained ankle. Several of those apprehended are wounded. Monsey has called for ambulances."

Maurice Monsey drove up in a police car with two officers. The officers ran to the two men on the ground. Monsey walked toward Gerard and Pierre. "You two know how to shoot. I'm impressed. This operation hit the jackpot. There's a lot of white powder in plastic bags behind the cardboard in these refrigerators. The customs inspector was arrested along with a fat envelope containing 100,000 Euros. Additional officers are arriving as we speak to inventory this stuff."

"Bon," said Gerard. "Now, we should begin interrogations of these people immediately, before they can collect their thoughts and get lawyers. I'll call my Italian counterpart. He'll probably want to participate in some of the questioning. He may also be able to apprehend the collaborators who are waiting in Italy for the shipments. Let's get to the truck drivers right away and see if they will reveal their destinations. Also, search the trucks and cars for maps and anything else of interest."

"I will see to it," said Monsey as he turned to go.

"Inspector Monsey," Gerard called.

"*Oui?*"

"Good work. You're the excellent cop Pierre said you were."

Monsey smiled broadly.

So did Pierre.

Chapter Thirty-One

PARIS

Laurent Gallet was excited as he hurried through the Place Saint-Michel and crossed to the Ile de la Cite. He hardly noticed the rain. The streetlights of Paris glowed orange through the growing, misty darkness.

Earlier that day the phone had rattled in his small apartment on the Rue des Ecoles. People seldom called him. This call was from a woman who said that she had information about some fraudulent paintings by the Russian artist, Ilia Dilinov. She knew he was an expert on Dilinov. It was information she wasn't supposed to have, and she wanted to meet him. His meeting with the police earlier that day had been useless. They would do nothing. He agreed to meet her.

As he crossed the bridge over the Seine, Gallet noticed the massive police headquarters building just across the street from the towers of Notre Dame, their lights shimmering through the mist. Holding his umbrella to fend off the rain, he headed down the stone stairs to the Quai next to the river. The Quai was deserted except for a dark-hooded figure standing against the wall.

His mind raced as he thought about his interview that morning with an officer of the French Art Police. *Maybe this woman will have information that will persuade this officer that the Dilinov paintings in that gallery on the Avenue Matignon are forgeries. As if my opinion isn't all that he needs. What a*

Philistine! The police won't do anything. Everyone in the art world knows that I am an expert on the works of this artist. I have studied the Russian painters of the 1930s for over forty years. This cop has probably never even seen a Dilinov painting. What a loss when he was killed in the War. This woman spoke French with a Russian accent. I wonder what her connection is to Dilinov. Well, I will soon find out.

Sofia Mostov checked the illuminated dial on her watch. *He will be on time. He seemed very anxious to talk with me when I told him I had information on the Dilinov paintings. He is the second old man I will have killed in a few months. He is an art scholar. Probably has led a quiet life in libraries and museums. I wonder if he has a family?*

The feel of the Beretta Cougar 800 in her skin-tight leather glove brought her out of her brief reverie. She tightened the suppressor on the barrel as she thought of the words many years ago of her KGB instructor. "You are never to be concerned about who you kill. Only how you kill. If you start thinking about who, your thoughts will soon progress to why. At that point, you are no longer an agent. You are a liability."

The old man with the umbrella walked down the stairs onto the Quai. He saw someone walking toward him out of the darkness. He heard a woman's voice. "Monsieur Gallet?"

He recognized her voice from the telephone conversation. "Oui, oui," he eagerly responded.

"Bon," she said. Then she looked around her once more, raised her hand and fired two shots into his head and one into his chest. He toppled backwards over the parapet into the river, his umbrella catching on the rail.

Sofia walked south on the island and threw the Beretta into the river.

Chapter Thirty-Two

Having taken the TGV back to Paris the afternoon of the Marseilles port arrests, Gerard was in his office the next morning.

Several senior officials came in to congratulate him. He told them to be sure to congratulate the Marseilles force.

"This is a chance to build a stronger cooperation with them."

One official said, "Talking about Marseilles, how long will Pierre be there?"

"At least one more day. I want him to be there when the Italian police do some of their questioning."

"Well, he must be happy. He got a chance to shoot someone. As did you. Gerard, you haven't lost your touch with a pistol," said another one of the officials. "Talking about shooting, have you heard that we pulled a body out of the river down near Boulogne-Billancourt? Three bullet holes in him."

"Have they identified him?"

"Yes, he had a wallet. Name is Gallet. Apparently some kind of art expert."

"I saw his name mentioned in a report a few days ago. He wanted to talk to a detective. That explains a call I got earlier this morning from one of the art fraud guys."

His visitors left and Gerard first returned a call from Steffani Terzazo. After a long conversation with Terzazo, who was flying to Marseilles from Rome later that morning, he then returned the call to the art fraud officer.

Accompanied by Louis Bordain, a young detective, Gerard went to the morgue to view the body of the man who had been pulled from the river. The medical examiner estimated that Gallet had been in the water about ten hours, which meant that he had been killed last night. The examiner said that with the wind and current he probably went into the river near the Île Saint-Louis.

"Louis, get some help and see if anyone heard shots or saw anything last night in the area on both sides of the river from the Pont de Sully to the Pont Notre Dame. I know it's a lot of territory but check with the cafes and bars. Maybe a waiter will recall something. Meanwhile, I'm going to meet with the art detective to see what he and Gallet talked about."

Chapter Thirty-Three

PARIS

Parking his BMW 650 in a no-parking area and placing a flashing red light on the dashboard, Gerard walked into the Gallery Libidoux. He had gotten the full report from the art fraud detective and was now going to talk with the gallerist himself.

Coming out of his office, Libidoux was surprised to see a distinguished-looking and well-dressed man in his lobby holding police identification.

Flustered, he said, "Are you here to see me?"

"Yes. I am Senior Inspector Gerard de Rochenoir of the French National Police, and I would appreciate a few minutes of your time."

"Of course, please come into my office."

Seated across from Libidoux, Gerard told him that he had been at the opening the previous week, and that he found the Dilinov paintings particularly interesting.

"Yes, a real talent. Tragic about dying so young. Very popular in Paris just before the war."

"Was this the first showing of this work?"

"No, the first showing was in Venice last month."

"Where was the Venice showing held?"

"At a new gallery there—the Gallery Perez. Mr. Perez is a Mexican collector who I believe has a house in Paris."

"Francesco Perez?"

"Yes, do you know him?"

"No, but I know of him. Do you and Mr. Perez have a business relationship that resulted in you getting the Dilinovs after him?"

Libidoux said, "Why are you asking me about this?"

Then Gerard asked, "Do you know Laurent Gallet?"

The abrupt change in the direction of his questioning had the desired effect. Libidoux snapped his head back, his mouth fell open, and he said, "The name is vaguely familiar, but I can't place him."

Gerard noticed beads of perspiration starting to appear on Libidoux's forehead. "Is it possible that he has visited your gallery?"

"It's possible. Many people come here."

"Is it possible that he came and met with you in the past few days? You would remember such a visit, wouldn't you?"

"Well, as I think about it someone did come to see me—perhaps his name was Gallet. It was a short visit."

"What was the subject of his visit?"

"He's interested in Russian art. But why are you asking me these questions?"

"Because Mr. Gallet was found this morning in the river—dead. He had been shot."

Libidoux sat silently and then said, "I am shocked to hear that."

"Mr. Libidoux, I would like you to come to my office tomorrow morning to continue this discussion. I will expect you at 10:00 AM. Here is my card with my office address. Don't get up. I can find my own way out."

After Gerard left, Libidoux sat in his office for a long time. He then called Perez.

"Francesco, we need to meet right away."

"What about?"

"I don't want to talk about it over the phone. I'm also going to call Sofia."

"She left for Venice this morning to meet Boris and attend the Biennale. I will meet you at three-thirty; I'll call you shortly with a location."

Chapter Thirty-Four

When Gerard entered the old black-timbered restaurant on the Rue Montorgueil, Marcel Lefour was already seated at a table facing the door.

Gerard looked at him through the restaurant window. *He never changes,* thought Gerard, *he reached eighty and then stopped looking older. He must have an inexhaustible supply of black berets, black sweaters, and black leather jackets.*

As a young courier for the Resistance who, because of his youth, could move about Paris relatively easily, it was Marcel who Gerard's father first met when he crept into Paris in August of 1944, and it was Marcel who told Gerard's mother about the rendezvous with her husband at the Café Deux Magots.

After the war, the young Marcel used his contacts to build a black-market business which evolved into a large fencing business. He spent a few years in prison where Gerard, now a policeman, met him. While professing to be retired he did maintain, as he sometimes put it, social contacts, with his former associates.

Gerard acted as his protector from overzealous cops and in return received valuable information about the goings on in the French underworld.

They often enjoyed a meal of escargot, Marcel's favorite, and this old restaurant was a haunt of theirs. As usual, Marcel was at the table, wearing his black beret and black sweater.

Marcel always got to the restaurant before Gerard, and Gerard always paid for the meal.

Gerard sat down at the table and ordered a dozen escargot prepared with Roquefort cheese for each of them and a bottle of Sancerre.

While Gerard thought that some Rieslings went well with escargot, he knew better than to order a German wine. Marcel never forgot his friends and never forgave his enemies.

"Good choice, Gerard, the snails are from Burgundy, so the wine should also be."

"You are looking good Marcel. Any news for me?"

"Well, you asked over the phone about Francesco Perez. I told you about him months ago when you were investigating those jewel robberies."

"And murders."

"Yes, but I found the jewel robberies more to my taste. Anyway, I did some checking. As I told you before, surprised as I was that an ace cop like you didn't know it, he's part of one of the big syndicates that moves white powder from Columbia through Mexico to the States. He's their business front, laundering cash for them through a number of legitimate enterprises."

"We searched his house during the previous investigation. Found nothing except a small arsenal. No drugs."

Marcel sopped up the sauce the snails came in with chunks of white bread. "This place has wonderful bread. Let's order some cheese."

Gerard signaled for the waiter.

"Did you know that Perez has been in Paris the past few weeks?"

Gerard shook his head no.

"I may have to join the force to help you out. In the Resistance and in my business after the war, we needed to know more than the other side or we would have been cooked like that lobster at the next table. Your father was a superb intelligence officer for de Gaulle. I would have thought some of his skill would have rubbed off on you."

Gerard smiled and shrugged his shoulders.

"Okay, Marcel, thank you for the obligatory negative comparisons with my father. I suppose you are going to tell me how he used to send back Stilton cheese in London restaurants."

"He did. Sent back their own cheese if it wasn't up to his own standards. And they invented the stuff. What a man he was." And then he made a rare smile. "But his son is pretty good too."

Marcel finished his first dozen escargot, and Gerard said, "Let's order some more. What about getting some with curry?"

"Okay with me. It's a specialty of this place."

Gerard ordered another two dozen snails and a bottle of Corton-Charlemagne, which he said was a better match with the curry.

As Marcel talked about the changing crime scene in Paris, "A lot of foreigners are getting involved," Gerard sat back and savored the spice of the curry contrasting with the snails in a butter and garlic sauce.

Reflecting on Marcel's comments about changes in Paris, he thought how comforting this old restaurant was to him. In Paris old restaurants and old men like Marcel didn't change. But, as he looked through the window at the shopping district that had replaced his beloved Les Halles, he thought, *but change and old age are inevitable. May they come gently.*

His reverie was interrupted by Marcel saying, "Perez has been seen with a woman who bears some resemblance to your Sofia Mostov. Those Russian spooks are very good at disguises."

"I wouldn't be surprised. She may have been spotted in Venice. So what do you hear Perez is up to? There have been no reports of increased drug activity in France."

"Is Marseilles still part of France?" Marcel said smiling.

"So you heard about our operation in Marseilles?"

"It isn't exactly a secret. The newspapers have run stories, although I see that you kept your name out."

"Better to let the Marseilles cops take the credit. Besides, after a slow start they have done a good job."

"And Abou shot one of the crooks?"

"Yes."

"Bless him."

"What do you think the connection is between these events in Marseilles and Perez?"

"I hear that the powder that was seized at the port was packed in refrigerators shipped from Mexico."

"Maybe," allowed Gerard.

"Did you know that one of the front businesses Perez runs for the syndicate in Mexico is appliance manufacturing?" Marcel said.

"No. We haven't started to investigate him yet."

"You better get started. One of the Italian families—the guys in the North—distribute appliances. It lets them move material around the country easily and clean some money."

"So, you think there's a connection between Perez and what I understand to be increased drug trafficking in Italy?" said Gerard.

"Suggest to Pierre that he put the question to Sherlock Holmes."

"I think I can figure out the answer. But I have another question, Marcel. Why do you think Perez has opened an art gallery in Venice?"

"How would I know? Maybe he has decided to give up a life of crime and devote himself to art. I don't get modern art anyway. I see stuff in gallery windows that my nieces and nephews could do."

"Probably," laughed Gerard. "But could they sell their work for millions of Euros?"

"Perhaps I'll try."

"Well, someone is making lots of money. Why not you too?" Gerard laughed and signaled for the bill. "Since we are talking about art, ask around and see if you can pick anything up about an art dealer named Marc Libidoux. He has a big gallery over on the corner of Matignon and Rue Saint-Honoré."

"Okay. And thanks for lunch."

Chapter Thirty-Five

"So, what are you going to say to this cop tomorrow?" asked Francesco Perez as he and Marc Libidoux sat at a corner table in a small bar on the far eastern end of Paris. "And you took a roundabout route here, right? It may be dangerous to be seen with you."

"You are not above this mess," Libidoux snapped. "This Gerard de Rochenoir knows that you showed the Dilinovs in Venice. He will probably pursue a connection between us."

Perez leveled a gaze at Libidoux, his eyes turning darker as he spoke. "There is no connection. Period. You must tell him that we have never met. The Russian collector, acting through his Swiss company, got in touch with you because of your interest in Russian art. And don't let the cop rattle you."

Libidoux was silent and then said, "I saw in the paper that there was a big drug bust at the Marseilles port."

"I read the papers."

"Are you in any kind of trouble?"

"I have never been to Marseilles, and I have told you not to ask me or talk about any of my other activities. No, I am not in trouble. You are the one being interviewed by a senior French cop. What are you going to say when he asks you about the authenticity of the Dilinovs?"

"I will say that the owner is satisfied with their authenticity."

"And when he asks you who the owner is?"

"Well, I could say that I don't know—there is a middle-man involved or that the owner desires that his name be kept confidential."

"Try both answers and then shut up. Be very careful what you say to the cop or the art expert will not be the last person who will be pulled out of the Seine. Do not call me again, and be careful what you say over the phone to anyone. Your office is not secure either. I'll be in touch."

With that, Perez got up and walked out into the street. Libidoux sat at the table, trying to keep his hands from shaking.

Chapter Thirty-Six

PARIS

Catherine York sat at her desk in the Paris offices of Larson and McTabbitt, gazing at the formal courtyard outside that led to the Avenue Matignon. She walked into the small kitchen and poured a cup of coffee thinking, *I should buy a coffee maker for the office, my stomach can't take much more of this strong French coffee.*

Then she picked up her phone and called her friend, Judy Weiss, in New York. Judy came on the line and, with her New York accent and direct manner, said, "Well I was wondering when I would hear from you. One e-mail since you got to Paris. I thought maybe you had run away with Gerard to some romantic place, but you are already in a romantic place. Still staying with him in his apartment?"

"Judy, at least you could have said hello before starting on the guilt trip."

"Okay. Hello. As your best friend, I worry when I don't hear from you. Besides, your life is a distraction for me from two kids, a lawyer-husband, and investment banking clients who seem to think I'm responsible for their stock price being down, although they have now missed two quarters of earnings projections. That's a capsule of my life. When you are radio silent for this long, it usually means something big is happening in your life. How is your work going? Actually, I don't care unless you got fired. What I really want to know is where you and Gerard are.'"

"It's a good thing that you took up investment banking as a career and didn't decide to be a therapist. You wouldn't have any clients."

Judy laughed and said, "I thought I would try the New York shtick on you. Are you okay?"

"I'm fine. I just need a little advice. Things are going very well between Gerard and me. We share his beautiful apartment. He likes my cooking. My work is interesting. Paris is wonderful, although I am spending too much money on clothes. Here's the situation. We now have met each other's families. That seems to have gone well. My parents and brothers really liked him. His sister and brother are very nice. But I'm here on a temporary assignment. I'm living with a man who is firmly embedded in his job and his life in Paris. I have an apartment in New York; most of my stuff is there as is my very good job. I can't stay here indefinitely."

Catherine stopped talking.

"Are you alright?" Judy said.

"I was just taking a sip of coffee. Funny, though, my impulse to call you—and I am so glad that I connected with you—was triggered by the thought that I really don't like the strong French coffee they have at the office and maybe I should buy myself a coffee maker."

"Well that would be an act of commitment. Let me change the subject slightly away from coffee makers. Do you love him? And does he love you?"

"We tell each other we do. But what does that mean?"

"It means a hell of lot for a commitment-challenged person like you."

"But could I live in Paris? What would a life in France be like? And then there is the age difference. Would he want kids? I'm too old to have kids. I have no friends here," Catherine's voiced trailed off into light sobs.

"Let it out, honey. Tears are cathartic at a time like this."

There was silence between the two friends. "If I were there with you, I would wipe your tears and hug you. It seems to me that you are getting ahead of yourself. That the two of you love each other is the most important thing. Damn it. It's the only thing. The two of you need to start envisioning what a life together would be like. There's no hurry. It sounds like you have plenty of work in Paris. You can try an across-the-Atlantic relationship, although my friends who do that say that it's stressful. Maybe he could work in the U.S. Didn't he spend two years in D.C. years ago? Maybe you could work permanently in France. Meanwhile, just enjoy the moments. You guys have plenty of money. If you're homesick, come back to New York for a week or so. Your parents could fly to Paris. Hey, maybe I'll come and visit you—that will shake things up!"

"Judy, I'd like to keep the job."

"All right, then. But do me one favor."

"What's that?"

"Buy the coffee maker."

Catherine laughed. "Thank you, thank you. I needed that. I have people waiting to meet with me, so I have to get off. This has meant a lot to me. Maybe you could have succeeded as a therapist."

"May I be spared such a career. I love you. Talk to you soon."

Chapter Thirty-Seven

When Gerard returned to the apartment that evening, as he opened the door a delicious smell of cooking was in the air. He went to the kitchen where Catherine, wearing a big apron over white jeans and a black t-shirt, was standing over the stove.

"You have changed the kitchen," he said.

"Only by adding some cooking utensils and decent knives. Otherwise, Gerard, I would change very little. I found an old shop over near the Louvre that has every kind of pan, duck press, and everything else for a Paris kitchen. This old kitchen, it's wonderful. And it's a marvelous contrast with the contemporary feel of the rest of the apartment, and the unit can be fitted with a large new refrigerator still keeping those heavy doors."

"It makes me happy that you appreciate this room. It holds many memories for me. Like the Wisconsin kitchen did for you.

"After my mother died, my sister and I decided that she and her family would continue to live in the family property in the south of France, and I would take over the apartment. At first I thought about selling it. I was living in east Paris, not far from the Picasso Museum, and it was a lively neighborhood—young people, music, cafés, and an art scene. But the more time I spent in this space, the more I realized that this was my only tie to my parents, and I became accustomed to living on this small island. So, I decided to—how would you say in English—remodel the place. I like the French word *remanier* better—it connotes more of a recasting which is what I tried to do. I changed no walls. I modernized the bathrooms. The beamed ceilings were repaired, but not changed. The big red marble fireplace you like so much was cleaned, but not changed. The colors of the plaster walls in the browns and off-white were not changed. I did replaster the library because of some damage. The parquet floors were refinished, and I replaced most of the furniture with more modern pieces—more to my taste. The windows and doors overlooking the river were repaired, but not otherwise changed. And since I don't cook, I made no changes in the kitchen."

"Gerard, it's a beautiful space, and I love cooking in this kitchen, although a more modern range would be a positive addition and there are models out there that wouldn't change the feel of the kitchen. I saw one at that shop I mentioned to you. But perhaps we're getting ahead of ourselves. I wouldn't want my staying here with you to be a forgone conclusion for either of us."

"You bring life and warmth to these old spaces." He kissed her and said, "That wonderful smell brings me back to my childhood in this apartment and the smells that came out of the kitchen."

"Did your mother cook a lot?"

"She did some cooking, and we had a chef who was quite good."

"What did your mother like to make?"

"Well, and this is a happy coincidence because of what you are preparing, she made a very good coq au vin."

"This may not be as good as hers, but I loved leaving work early and visiting several small shops on the island to buy a chicken, vegetables, and other ingredients. A big difference from American supermarkets."

Gerard took a forkful of chicken and said, "This is

wonderful, and you have addressed the two big issues facing chefs who make coq au vin—a tasty sauce and chicken that's tender."

"The recipe for my sauce is a secret. A girl can't reveal everything. But when I prepare the chicken, I first brown it in olive oil, and I had to buy some regular olive oil since all you had was extra virgin which is too strongly flavored for my sauce. I leave the skin on a bone-in chicken breast, sear it so the skin is brown, then I rest it on a plate while I sauté onions, shallots, a bundle of fresh thyme, garlic, and salt and pepper. Then I add dry white wine and fresh chicken stock, which I made this afternoon, bring it to a boil, add the chicken, and put the covered pot into the oven at a low temperature for three hours. That's why I had to leave the office so early—a lot of shopping and preparation."

"This is a very good dish. It's different from traditional French coq au vin, which is usually made with a rooster and red wine."

"Thank you. I have perhaps Americanized the dish."

"Your sauce is special, so we can call this *Coq Au Vin à la Catherine*."

"Another example of contrasting American and French approaches to things. I probably will never do classical French cooking, but I will try to respect it as I work on my cooking. And I can always consult recipes. But, I like my chicken tender and the milder flavor of white meat. The classic preparation uses dark meat, but I guess my preference for white meat is very American. White wine seemed to work better than red. Another American modification. Would I be insulting French cuisine if I described my approach as more modern than the traditional preparation?"

"I like your spontaneity, experimentation, American ingenuity, and fearlessness."

"Wow. Well, that is who I am. But I'm also hard working—you forgot that in your list of adjectives."

"How are things going at your office?"

"Not well," Catherine sighed. "They seem to think their role is to process paper. Investigative rigor is not their strength. The manager was prepared to pay a multi-million Euro claim in Belgium from a boiler explosion without looking into the question of fraud and, more likely, negligence. I'm going through all open files."

"It sounds like you'll be in Paris for a while."

"Probably. Are you going to kick me out of the apartment?"

"No. And I agree that we should consider some changes to the kitchen."

"That was a good answer."

Over dinner Gerard told Catherine about the murder of Laurent Gallet.

"That name is familiar," Catherine said and got up from the table to get notes out of her brief case. "He was on a list of experts I wanted to consult in connection with the insurance on the paintings at Gallery Libidoux."

"Didn't you say that you were insuring the paintings that we saw at the opening there a couple of evenings ago? Incidentally, I'm not going to any more art openings with you. They're too dangerous."

"From what I hear took place down in Marseilles, you have enough excitement in your life. You didn't say much to me about it."

"I didn't want to worry you, although that turned out to be quite a melee."

"Pierre said that you saved his life."

"Perhaps."

"Why do you ask about insurance on the paintings at Libidoux's gallery?"

"I was looking at our log and noticed that someone came into one of the Paris police offices, said he was an art expert and wanted to talk to the police about fraudulent paintings by an artist named Dilinov. The guy's name was Gallet. He was supposed to meet today with one of our art cops. He was killed last night."

"Why would anyone want to kill an eccentric old art scholar?"

"We're just starting our investigation. He lived alone. No immediate family. It wasn't a robbery—his wallet and watch were on the body. But we know this from what he told one of our officers the morning of the murder. He was suspicious of the authenticity of the Dilinov paintings at the Libidoux gallery as well as works of another Russian artist named Yevgeny. He met with Libidoux who dismissed his suspicions. And he got a call from an unidentified woman who said she had information about the Dilinovs and wanted to meet with him."

"So the Dilinovs are part of this?"

"It would seem so. Another person who is somehow involved is a Mexican drug figure by the name of Francesco Perez. His name came up earlier this year in connection with the Sofia Mostov matter, and he has a gallery in Venice that displayed the Dilinovs before they came to Paris."

"And don't we think that the thugs who tried to kidnap me in Miami were connected to Mexican gangsters?"

"Yes, the Miami police were sure of that. Also, the Mexican connection has surfaced in connection with a plot to bring cocaine and heroin into Europe through Marseilles, move it to Italy, and distribute it. So, we have a Mexican-Italian nexus. Is Perez involved? Are we going to encounter Sofia Mostov again? And what is behind this art business? There are pieces to be pulled together.

"Your insurance suspicions may be well founded. Didn't you say that the art that Libidoux is showing and that Perez apparently had in his Venice gallery was being insured by a Swiss insurance company?"

"I did. The art is supposedly owned by a Russian collector who operates through Swiss corporations. I suppose that's why the primary coverage originated in Switzerland."

"Libidoux is coming to my office tomorrow. I'll try to get more out of him. The motive for the Gallet killing may be found somewhere in the world of Perez, Libidoux, and maybe even Sofia Mostov."

"Sofia? Why do you think that?"

"It was a woman with whom Gallet was to meet the night he was killed."

Chapter Thirty-Eight

PARIS

Gerard stood at the window of his office looking out over Notre Dame.

"Your favorite place to stand these days," said Pierre Abou.

"This job involves too much sitting. Marseilles reminded me of my younger days in the field."

"It was a successful operation. The Mexicans aren't talking at all—yet the one I shot is still in the hospital. I wonder if we can charge him with attempted murder for trying to impale me on a front loader."

"You shoot well when your life is in danger."

"It does focus one's aim. My Italian is lacking, but from what I can tell and from what our interpreter told me, Terzazo got a lot out of one of the Italians."

"He now has a clear idea of who is involved on the Italian side. We should plan on going to Italy soon to meet with him. Meanwhile, I have this art dealer coming in shortly."

"Do you think he had something to do with Gallet's murder?"

"He doesn't seem the type to pull the trigger, but yes, I think he knows much more than he's saying. We need both Sherlock Holmes and Marcel to help us figure this one out. I'm seeing Marcel later today for a drink."

•   •   •

Marc Libidoux was disoriented as an unsmiling woman led him through the drab corridors of police headquarters into Gerard's warm and pleasant office.

Gerard was standing, looking out of a window. He turned and pointed Libidoux to a chair in front of his desk. As Libidoux sat down, he looked up and saw a large display of handcuffs on the wall behind the desk. Gerard positioned himself so they remained visible over his shoulder.

"I understand that you are having trouble getting insurance coverage on the pieces in your show," said Gerard. "Is that because of questions of authenticity?"

"No. No. But how do you know about the insurance?" Libidoux fussed, trying without success to find a comfortable perch on the small wooden chair Gerard had switched with his more comfortable furniture just before Libidoux's arrival.

"Isn't it true, Mr. Libidoux, that if your insurance carrier knew of Laurent Gallet's suspicions about the Dilinovs, they wouldn't have covered you?"

"But the Dilinovs are authentic."

"How can you be so sure? What investigation did you undertake?"

"I talked with the Russian collector, and I talked with the Venice gallery owner who showed the Dilinovs before I did."

"And who is this Russian collector?"

"I can't reveal that."

"Do you know who he is?"

"No I don't. He wants to remain anonymous."

"If he is anonymous, how could you have talked with him?"

Shifting his weight in his chair, "I'm very uncomfortable answering these questions."

"No doubt. So you discussed the Dilinov paintings with Francesco Perez?"

"I never asked him if the Dilinovs were authentic."

"What have you discussed with him?"

"I hardly know him."

"When did you last meet with him?"

"I have never met with him. We covered some logistics for shipping paintings over the phone."

"So, you did not meet with him at a café yesterday afternoon?"

"No."

"Mr. Libidoux, lying to a police officer is a crime. Would it help your memory if I gave you the name of the café? Or if I showed you a picture of the two of you there together?"

Still squirming, Libidoux finally slumped in his chair, deflated. Gerard thought he looked like a large balloon that had lost its helium. The balloon was now sweating.

"I didn't kill Gallet. I don't know anything about what happened to him. Yes, I met with him. That's all. I think I need to talk with a lawyer before I can answer any more questions."

"Why did you pull the Monet from the Sidney Pebbles' auction?"

"Provenance questions. But I want to talk to a lawyer."

"You can talk to a lawyer—that's your right. But you are not to leave Paris, and we will schedule a hearing for you shortly. Detective Bordain will explain the process to you."

He then pressed a buzzer and Louis Bordain came in, put his arm on Libidoux, and led him out of Gerard's office. Gerard never looked up from the papers on his desk.

◆　◆　◆

Next morning, picking up the phone in his office, Gerard said, "Good morning, Pierre. What's the news from Marseilles?"

"Marseilles is lovely as always. As for the case, the Mexicans won't talk, but they carried the kinds of guns that were used in both of the port murders. We're checking ballistics, but there is enough to hold them on several charges."

"Including trying to kill a policeman," Gerard said.

"I'm sure Monsey doesn't think that such an act should be

punished if I am the policeman."

"I thought you decided he had improved."

"He wasn't particularly cooperative with Terzazo."

"Monsey probably doesn't like Italians," Gerard said. "Particularly well-dressed ones who speak perfect French."

"How did your discussion with Marcel go yesterday?"

"He still has a big appetite for escargot and expensive wine, as long as it's French. His sources confirm that Perez and his people have stayed out of moving their stuff into France, but they doubt that he will remain out of the game here for long. Italy is another matter. The word is that he has spent a lot of time there."

"So, what's our next move?"

"I put surveillance on both Perez and Libidoux yesterday morning right after I visited Libidoux at his gallery. They met in the afternoon, then Perez flew to Venice. Terzazo's people are watching him."

"Can we tie him to the Gallet murder?"

"Not yet, but I'm sure there is a connection to the Dilinovs. Also someone found a nine-millimeter casing on the quai below the Saint-Michel bridge and actually gave it to a gendarme. It appears that it matched one of the bullets that stayed in Gallet. He had some kind of metal plate in his head, so the bullet never exited. They also found an umbrella on the quai that may have belonged to Gallet."

"So, he was shot a few meters from our headquarters?"

"It appears so."

"Is someone taunting us?"

"Maybe. Or maybe a coincidence."

"No coincidence that the shooter didn't pick up the bullet casings, or the umbrella. What do we do next?"

"Spend as much time today as you can interrogating the prisoners. The Mexicans could help us—and the Italians will probably implicate the Mexicans with enough persuasion."

"We're following that path."

"Good, meanwhile we will start the process of seizing the art from Libidoux's gallery and seeing if we can make a determination as to its authenticity, but it will take a while. Catherine is now involved because the insurance companies she works for insured the Dilinovs as well as Libidoux's other art for a lot of money. The Dilinovs he has are alone insured for over seven million Euros. With enough persuasion, Libidoux will talk, although Perez has probably frightened him. We're watching him closely, both because we don't want him to vanish or to be hit. These Mexican gangsters tend to act quickly and harshly and if Sofia Mostov is involved—well, between the two of them, Libidoux is in real danger. Call me at the end of the day. Good luck with your questioning."

◆ ◆ ◆

"We are making progress," said Pierre, calling Gerard from Marseilles later in the afternoon. "The Italians thought that they would be extradited to Italy, so they were keeping quiet—apparently the prospect of being returned to Italy didn't frighten them much, but I told them that they would remain in France and be prosecuted for murder. I even wore my National Police uniform during the questioning."

"All that gold braid must have scared them," Gerard said.

"One of the truck drivers cracked first. He's pretty low level and implicated the tall guy as the boss. We worked the truck driver hard. He denied knowing anything about the murders but admitted that they had picked up several loads of appliances—refrigerators and microwaves—over the past few months and had driven them into Italy where the drugs were unloaded. The appliances were then trucked to Genoa. They gave us locations where the drugs were unloaded.

"Then we worked the tall guy. He said he would give us more information on the Mexicans and details of the dockyard murders, if we would drop the murder charges and extradite him to Italy."

"Did he?" said Gerard.

"He first denied knowing anything about the murders, but finally said that the Mexicans killed the two guys from Naples because they were spying on the transfer at the dockyards. He said that he didn't know anything about the killing of the dockyard workers."

"Progress indeed, Pierre. I'll call Terzazo and see how he wants to handle the next step. What else?"

"Nothing, except for a visit from the Mexican consulate. We talked to the people at the hotel where the Mexicans were staying. There was apparently a third man but he has skipped. I have his description, and we will circulate it. We found two bags in a locker at the train station—nothing much except Mexican and Venezuelan passports, Euros, and spare magazines for their Predators. They claim to understand no French or English and the Spanish-speaking Marseilles cops as well as our Spanish-speaking colleague can get nothing out of them. The guy I shot has an arm in a sling and a brace around his shoulder. He stares at me."

"You may have to shoot him again."

"Is that an order?"

"Unofficial."

They both laughed.

"Anything more on the Gallet murder?" said Pierre.

"No," sighed Gerard. "Libidoux has an alibi for the night of the shooting. He was at an opening at the d'Orsay. But my meeting him at his gallery worked. He was scared. We were watching both he and Perez. Libidoux met with Perez as fast as he could and then denied the meeting. We caught him lying about his connection to Perez, and after that he crumbled pretty fast. He now admits to telling Perez about Gallet's suspicions that the paintings were not authentic. I pushed him, and he finally said that he also told Sofia Mostov. He's been working with Perez, Boris Vorshilov, and Sofia Mostov on selling paintings that Boris and Sofia have access to in

Moscow. He claims he thought they were all authentic, but acknowledges that they have a 'restorer,' as he describes him, who works with them. Whoever this person is, I think he's a lot more than a restorer.

"Well, Gerard, that's progress. But unless the art is stolen, it isn't a crime to sell art."

"My guess is that some of this art was stolen—probably by the Nazis during the war—so any attempt to sell it would raise the provenance disputes that continue to roil the art market. I talked with the director at Sidney Pebbles, the new auction house here in Paris, and he says that Libidoux pulled a Monet from their last auction because of concerns over provenance. The painting was in his gallery, and we have experts looking at it. It may be genuine. Now where did he get a Monet?"

"Perhaps it's fake?" said Pierre.

"It's a crime to knowingly sell fakes as originals, and we have enough to hold Libidoux on that. We are also checking his bank accounts. He's scared of Perez and wants us to protect him. I told him that if he wants protection, he has to give us more. I don't think he knows that we're keeping him under surveillance. We'll try to find the Mexican who was working with the guys you have in custody, but we need more of a description."

"Where is Perez, now?"

"Terzazo says that Perez is now in Venice at his gallery and there have been possible Sofia Mostov sightings in Venice. The mysterious Boris may be there as well. Perez has a big boat in Venice that he's been using to go back and forth to Montenegro. The Italian police are watching the boat. You and I need to go to Venice in the next few days."

Chapter Thirty-Nine

A young Swiss employee of Larsen and McTabbitt, assigned to work with Catherine on open claims, knocked on her office door.

"Come in, Albert," she said, thinking that she liked his crisp, orderly Swiss manner. He was the only executive she had seen in her three weeks in the Paris office who worked through lunch and ate at his desk. "What's up?"

Albert gave a half smile and said, "Madame York, in addition to much I don't know about claims investigations and risk assessment that I am learning from you, I also am improving my English by learning your colloquialisms. But what do you mean by 'up?'"

"Why, Albert, what I mean is that I'm glad to see you, and what brings you to my office?"

"Ah—what you call shorthand."

"Well—sort of."

"I just got a call from the art dealer we visited—Marc Libidoux."

"Is he still complaining about our meeting when I told him that we would only agree to a two-week binder until we resolved the provenance of the paintings?"

"No, he has a more serious problem, Madame York, and perhaps we do as well. He has closed his gallery. He says it's to address some personal issues. Seems he's a bit shaken.

"Yesterday afternoon Libidoux says he opened because someone was interested in purchasing some work. While he waited in his office, he had heard shouting and found a man slashing some of the Dilinov paintings and shouting that the Russians were barbarians who had murdered his family in Berlin during the war and their art should be destroyed. Libidoux tried to stop him, but he was shoved aside and the man ran out of the gallery."

"Amazing. Did he call the police?"

"Yes, they eventually arrived, got a description of this guy, and took a few pictures of the damage. They haven't apprehended the person yet."

"And Libidoux only now called us?"

"Yes, he says that he was too shaken to call us earlier."

"Albert, call his primary carrier in Geneva. I'm sure that they will want us to do the investigation, but confirm it. Then call Libidoux and tell him not to move anything or clean anything up. Leave the paintings on the wall. Tell him that we will come to the gallery in about an hour."

Later, as they sat in Catherine's office, Albert said. "So, Madame York, you don't believe Libidoux?"

"Please, call me Catherine, and no, I don't believe him. I think he lied to us for an hour. Here is what I think happened. Libidoux slashed the Dilinovs himself. Doing so made it very difficult to ascertain whether they are fakes or not."

"What makes you think that he slashed the paintings?"

"Did you notice anything suspicious about the damage to the paintings?"

"Not really—they were certainly heavily damaged."

"That's the point. My friend—*what else do I call him*, thought Catherine—is a senior detective in Paris, and his assistant is a Sherlock Holmes fan. At lunch a few days ago, this assistant referenced a story where Holmes made the distinction between seeing and observing. We both saw the damage, but I observed that the paintings were quite methodically cut up. The angry German who Libidoux claimed slashed the paintings would have, in his rage, taken big swipes with his knife. I asked Libidoux how long this angry German was alone with the paintings. You remember what he said?"

"Just a few minutes."

"Correct. And how did Libidoux describe the knife the guy had?"

"He said it was big—like a butcher's knife."

"Yes, he did. But the cutting was finer than what would have resulted from a big knife and the slashes were methodical—both horizontal and vertical. And why would the slasher cut the artist's signature at the very bottom of the paintings?"

"I don't know."

"Because it takes a lot of practice to forge a signature, particularly an elaborate one like Dilinov's—walk over to the d'Orsay and see the Dilinov hanging there and look at his signature. It's very complex.

"And of course the police have not been able to find anyone matching the description Libidoux gave of this criminal. Add in the fact of the unfortunate, but timely death, at least from Libidoux's point-of-view, of poor Mr. Gallet. But we do know what the leading Dilinov expert in Paris thought about the Libidoux Dilinovs because he met with one of the detectives on the French force who specializes in art crime and told him that the Dilinovs were fakes. The night of that meeting he is murdered. An amazing coincidence, don't you think?"

Nodding his head, Albert asked Catherine if the company was going to pay the claim Libidoux was making.

Frowning, Catherine said, "I only make recommendations. But if Libidoux damaged his own paintings in such a manner as to make authentication difficult, then he knew that they were fakes." He would be committing the crime of selling a work of art as genuine when he knew it was not. As well as making a fraudulent insurance claim. Not only would we not pay his claim under these circumstances, he would be in trouble with the police.

"But I think something even bigger is going on. Your research into the origin of some of the paintings Libidoux included on his application for insurance was excellent. As you pointed out, a number of those works disappeared during the war, and they have never resurfaced, nor are they on the lists of works recovered by the Americans after the war."

"The Monuments Men they were called," said Albert.

"Right. They did important work and their records can be helpful to us. Now some of the paintings Libidoux has are coming out of Russia, so it's logical that they were seized by the Russians and are now being sold, apparently through Libidoux and maybe this Venice gallery."

"But where does the apparent forgery of the Dilinovs fit in?"

"I don't know for sure, Albert, but I'm developing a theory. And I think it's time that our investigation and the work being done by the French police be carried on jointly."

"A good idea, but how can you make that happen?"

Catherine smiled.

Chapter Forty

The sun streamed into the kitchen of Gerard's apartment on the Isle St. Louis as Gerard and Catherine sat at the kitchen table.

"I'm still getting used to what you call breakfast," Catherine said, holding up a flaky croissant. "I need something more substantial." She set a plate full of scrambled eggs and bacon in front of Gerard.

"And you are converting me to the American concept of breakfast. Large portions."

"I have another American custom that I want to introduce you to—the breakfast meeting."

"Hmm. Seems very uncivilized."

Catherine then described her visit to the Gallery Libidoux the previous day and her conclusion that Libidoux had staged the slashing of the Dilinov paintings to cover up the forgeries.

Gerard listened intently. "Very interesting. That poor fellow, Gallet, seemed quite certain that the Dilinovs were frauds. I finally got the report from the art fraud cop on his meeting with him. I will get you a copy, but Gallet's comments are quite persuasive, and he was an expert on this Russian artist."

"There is more, Gerard. We looked into the background of some of the paintings that Libidoux wanted to insure. They are owned by this mysterious Russian collector with the Swiss company. It's likely that they were seized in France, Holland, and Belgium by the Nazis. Then they disappeared, and have only recently begun to resurface, coming out of Russia. And now this." Catherine reached to a side table and put a copy of the catalogue from the recent Sidney Pebbles' auction on the table. Opening it up, she said, "Look at this Monet. It was put in the auction by Libidoux but withdrawn before the auction. One of the executives in our office knows someone at the auction house and called to ask why the Monet didn't go to auction. He was told because the provenance was murky. But the auction house believes it to be a genuine Monet. It hadn't been seen since it was seized in Paris by the Germans. Now it comes out of Russia. Did the Russians take it from the Germans? Otherwise how would it have gotten to Russia?"

Gerard responded, "I know about this painting that Libidoux put into the Sidney Pebbles' auction. It's a very well-known Monet. Libidoux is no fool. Why would he put it into the auction knowing that the provenance issue would very likely come up? And then agree to withdraw it, but make a point of asking the auction house to get the word out that the withdrawal was for provenance reasons rather than questions of authenticity?"

Catherine tapped her finger. "The director at Sidney Pebbles who spoke to my associate mentioned that Libidoux put up only token resistance to the withdrawal, but that the director was surprised that he even brought up the authenticity question since the auction house never raised it."

"The obvious answer, Catherine, is that Libidoux wanted to protect the value of the Monet. But, as Pierre mentioned to me recently, Sherlock Holmes once said something to the effect of 'nothing is more misleading than an obvious fact.'"

"Okay, if the obvious fact is that his reason for withdrawing the Monet was to protect its value, what is misleading?"

Catherine and Gerard were silent as they contemplated Catherine's question. Then, almost simultaneously, they looked at each other and nodded their heads. Gerard spoke first.

"What he was trying to do was not so much to protect the Monet's value, since he knew it was authentic and would hold its value in the future, but…"

Catherine finished his sentence, "to reinforce the reputation of this anonymous Russian as the source of high value and authentic art."

"And," Gerard said, "so that forgeries sold by Libidoux from this Russian's collection would be more readily accepted as genuine." He exhaled. "Catherine, I am now a convert to breakfast meetings—at least with you."

"What's the next step?"

"Another piece of the puzzle is that we have discovered that large sums of money have come into Mr. Libidoux's accounts over the past few months. He has used these funds to buy paintings—get this—from Russia. The deposits were in dollars and Euros. The money was routed primarily through Switzerland and the Cayman Islands, but our people think it originated in Mexico, the United States, and Italy. Some of it came through Francesco Perez's new gallery in Venice. The origin of these funds is very suspicious."

"Gerard, your eggs are cold."

"Cold eggs are the result of a breakfast meeting where a great deal of information is put on the table. We now have a melange of murders, art fraud, insurance fraud, and money laundering. Add drug smuggling and drug distribution in Italy and that is quite a meal to digest.

"We will put Libidoux on a short leash and continue to question him today. Then Pierre and I will go to Venice to see Señor Perez."

Chapter Forty-One

"Steffani, you pick not only churches, but ones with great art for our meetings."

"Ettore, the veracity of what you tell me is enhanced by the holy places where the conversations take place. Besides, here at Santa Maria del Carmine you can look up at Masaccio's *Adam and Eve Expelled from Paradise* and contemplate the consequences of not doing the right thing for Italy."

Grassi removed a large envelope from his satchel and handed it to Terzazo. "It's all here. The details of the Mexican plan to take over the Italian drug trade."

"Thank you. A lesson for you about the danger of partners. I'm sure your father would agree. No more globalization of your business. It's dangerous and not in the best interest of the patria."

"When will my men be released by the French?"

"If they indeed committed no murders, soon. Study the painting over there of St. Peter distributing alms to the poor. Charity is good for the soul. Greet your father for me."

When Grassi turned around, the Assistant Commissioner was gone.

Chapter Forty-Two

The phone woke Perez from a sound sleep. He answered it as the sun streamed in through the windows of his suite at the Hotel Danieli, overlooking the Grand Canal. Still groggy, Perez said hello and heard the unmistakable gravelly voice of El Gordo.

"Perez, can you hear me?"

"Yes, you are in Mexico? It must be afternoon there."

"Never mind where I am. Just listen to me. We just heard from one of our contacts in Naples that the Italian National Police are on to you and are going to arrest you. Do you have an escape plan?"

"No. But I will come up with something."

El Gordo muttered an obscenity. "You had better. You don't have much time."

The line went dead.

Perez climbed out of his bed and looked through the windows of his suite at the Riva degli Schiavoni below. Crowded as usual he could see no police presence. He crept to the door of his suite and looked up and down the hallway. Nothing out of the ordinary. He stood in his pajamas. His body and mind seemed frozen.

What was I thinking? I let myself get so absorbed in this city and in my identity as a gallery owner that I let my guard down. At least I should have brought Diego with me. OK, Francesco,

*pull yourself together. You're on an island and you must get off
of it. Why are the police after me? It can't be the art. They must
have found out about the drug business. But how? I have been
so careful.*

Moving quickly, he grabbed a small shoulder bag he used
for traveling. Then he put on a pair of pants and a shirt. Still
barefoot, he opened the room safe and removed his passport
and a thick envelope of Euros. He also took out a Berretta
Colt 32 caliber automatic and an extra clip and put it into the
bag. He put on his shoes and a light jacket.

*What else will I need? You have money and your passport.
Dummy, you are not packing for a trip! You have to get out of
the hotel. They will know where you are staying. Move quickly.
But where to?*

He took the passport, money, and pistol out of the overnight bag, put them in the pockets of his jacket, and walked
to the door of the room. Remembering that he had forgotten
his watch and wallet, he went back into the room. He looked
out of the windows again and saw a police car parked on the
Riva. Something he hadn't seen since he had been in Venice.

Leaving his room, he walked down the service steps to the
hotel basement where the hotel workers changed into their
uniforms.

A hotel janitor said in Italian, "Are you lost? Can I help
you?"

"Si. Where is the exit?"

The janitor turned to open the door and pointed in the
direction down the basement corridor to an exit. It was the
last thing he remembered as Perez, having seen a crow bar in
a tool closet, came up behind him and hit him twice on the
back of his head. He then took off the janitor's grey, stained
workman's jacket and his equally stained cap, transferred the
contents of his cashmere and silk jacket to the pockets of the
janitor's jacket, and walked into the corridor.

Several other hotel workers were leaving the hotel as the

night shift ended, and Perez hunched over and tried to blend in with them as they walked out of the rear service door. As he made his way around the hotel to the Riva, he saw two policeman, carrying automatic weapons, position themselves at the back of the hotel.

Reaching the Riva, he saw another police car and a police boat idling in the canal. More police were at both ends of the Riva, and he thought they might be setting up barricades.

I don't want to get trapped here, he said to himself. I'll take a water taxi.

He walked along the Riva, waving at the few water taxis cruising by. None paid any attention to him. He took off his janitor's cap and started waving a 50 Euro note. Becoming increasingly desperate, he saw a long wooden row boat, with fading green paint and a small outboard motor close to the entrance of a small canal just beyond the hotel. He shouted to the boatman.

"I will miss my train, 50 Euros to take me to the station."

As the boat pulled up, the boatman said, "100 Euros." Perez climbed in and gave him the money. The first thing he noticed was the smell. Then he saw the cans. The boat was hauling garbage, he realized.

The boat headed into the Grand Canal and turned toward San Marco. Then Perez saw the police boat that had been in front of the Danieli coming toward them. The boatman, facing forward, did not see the police boat, but he did see Perez try to lie down on the floor of the boat. He then heard the voice of an officer on the boat ordering him to take the boat back to the small canal. He looked down at Perez who was pointing a gun at him and saying take the boat to San Marco. Looking at the rapidly approaching police boat and then down at Perez and the gun, he killed the engine on the boat and jumped into the canal.

The police boat threw a floating ring to the boatman and came aside the garbage boat. With two officers pointing automatic weapons at him and his boat now tethered to the police boat, Perez dropped his pistol and raised his hands. A few minutes later, he was handcuffed and an unhappy passenger on a police boat taking a short ride to the Questura.

Chapter Forty-Three

"That was the most expensive breakfast I've ever had," Pierre said. "Almost one hundred Euros for two croissants, an orange juice, and coffee. Now we have walked through narrow, twisting streets, over bridges that don't lead anywhere, and through groups of tourists following a guide with an umbrella like a flock of sheep. I'm not sure I like Venice."

"Pierre, it's an acquired taste, but we have reached the Questura."

They were shown to a conference room where Terzazo and his team had set up a small command post. Terzazo was on a radio. His men were searching for Sofia Mostov.

"Good morning, gentlemen," Terzazo said, his voice revealing his excitement. "We are watching a pensione near the Querini Stampalia where we think she is staying. The desk clerk has identified her picture, although she has apparently dyed her hair. His radio crackled again and Terzazo said, "Sofia Mostov has left her pensione and is walking toward the Campo San Provalo." He pointed toward a large map of Venice on the wall.

"We have several officers in plain clothes tracking her and radioing in." He continued to report on what he was hearing from the police following her, and indicating her position on the map.

"She's headed north again past the San Zaccaria Church. She's crossing the bridge over the San Lorenzo Canal. She's looking around. She's joining a crowd of tourists. She may suspect something. She's only a few hundred meters from the Questura."

Terzazo said to the senior Venetian officer in the room, "You better change followers. I'm sure that she's quite skilled at detecting surveillance." He turned to Gerard, "Now she's taken off a black head scarf and put on a pair of large sunglasses."

Pierre asked, "What else is she wearing?"

Terzazo talked into his radio. "Black slacks, a black sweater, and a baseball-style cap. Wait. She's going in the direction of Perez's gallery. They have momentarily lost sight of her, but she seems to have headed south, in the direction of the canal. Wait a minute." Terzazo pressed the handset to his ear, "Speak up, I can't hear you. Okay. Good work. We've arrested Perez. He's now in a cell in this building."

"Good! Pierre, call Monsey in Marseilles and give him the news. He might want to inform his Mexican prisoners that Perez has been arrested in Italy and is implicating them. They might then start to cooperate."

Terzazo said that one of the Venice officers would continue to report on Sofia's progress. He was going to greet Perez.

After a few minutes, the officer said, "Okay. We have her again. It's crowded, but they are observing her walk along the canal. She just passed the Palazzo Gabrieli. With the opening of the Biennale, it's getting very crowded where she is. She has stopped at the Restaurant San Giorgio and has taken a table on the terrace. What? She got up from the table and went into the restaurant. She hasn't come back to the table. I think she's spotted her followers."

The Venice police officer following the reports over the radio said to Gerard and Pierre, "Our people just searched her room at the pensione where she was staying. She wasn't planning to leave since she hadn't packed. There was some literature on the Biennale in her room. Perhaps she's planning to visit it today. She's heading in that direction."

"That's a good surmise," said Gerard. "Even if that wasn't her plan, I'm sure she knows that she's under surveillance, and if she wants to lose herself she'll go where there are large crowds, and that's the Biennale. Call Terzazo and ask him to come up."

Shortly, Terzazo entered the command center saying, "Perez is doing the irate act, so we're letting him cool down in a depressingly small cell."

"Sofia seems to be trying to elude the police," Gerard said. "Can we intercept her at the Biennale?"

"It's very crowded. What do you suggest, comandante?" Terzazo asked the Venice police chief who had joined them.

"I can send officers with a description of her to the Biennale, and we can go there quickly by police launch. I suggest that we use the officers who are following her as posts on both bridges over the Rio dell'Arsenale. That should seal her off."

"Okay, let's get on that launch," said Terzazo.

As the French and Italian police disembarked from the police launch, Gerard surveyed the scene and thought to himself, *this is a big area with ticket booths, restaurants, many pavilions and large crowds. It won't be easy to find her.* The Venice chief led Gerard, Pierre, Terzazo, and two of his men to an unmarked gate. He distributed radios to each, along with maps of the Biennale. "I've called for a number of additional officers. I'll wait here to instruct them when they arrive. We already have a good number here as part of Biennale security, and we're alerting them as well. It's a large area, but we have a good chance of finding Sofia."

Pierre studied his map and said to Gerard, "She's going to be hard to find here. All these buildings—many of them old with multiple entrances—the crowds. This will not be easy."

As they entered the Biennale, the Venetian policeman accompanying them pointed to a large white building to the left of the VIP gate and said, "That's the Central Pavilion, where a large crowd is waiting to enter. We can go in through a special door and look around quickly."

As they walked into the building, Pierre asked, "Where is the art here?"

Gerard responded, "Those illustrated manuscripts are the art, Pierre. They're the works of a famous Swiss psychologist who worked on them for many years."

"But what are they?"

"They are self-induced visions that he called *The Red Book.*"

"They don't look like art to me."

Looking around at the large room, Gerard said, "Pierre, this isn't the time to discuss that question. They are his meditations and dreams. A theme that I understand persists through this Biennale. But Sofia isn't here, so let's keep going."

The Venetian policeman's radio crackled, "She has been seen in the Venice Pavilion." Pushing their way through crowds, the Venetian cop holding his badge up above his head, they reached one of the older buildings on the grounds. Motioning them to enter, he pointed to a crowd standing in front of a large mural depicting a number of figures in varied forms of dress on a marble staircase, an oriental building in the background, and three sculpted lions overlooking the scene. As the crowd, apparently part of a tour group, moved on, they caught a glimpse of a woman dressed in black and wearing a baseball cap.

As they tried to wedge their way through both departing and arriving tour groups, they exited the building. "No sign of her," said Pierre, "but I think she's discarded her cap," pointing to a cap with a Venetian lion on it lying on the ground.

A uniformed policeman joined them and said, "I think she's headed to the Spanish Pavilion."

As the policemen, now four in number, approached a modernist white building, another officer was talking on her radio and pointed to the entrance. "The place is falling apart," explained Pierre, looking at the rooms full of rubble. "We can't even get into these rooms."

"Well, Pierre, neither can she. We can come back some other time to understand the message this artist is sending by filling these rooms with rubble. But let's get out of here—she won't stay. She will be too visible."

A call came in that she had been seen walking in front of the United States' Pavilion. One of the Venetian officers said, "She has apparently changed her baseball-style cap for a head scarf."

The Venetian cops were trying to cover the ground in some kind of order, but the crowds, the twisting walkways, and the multiple entrances and exits of the pavilions made their task difficult. The grounds of the Biennale included some of the old shipyards where the ships of the legendary Venetian fleet had been built.

Along a lagoon at one end of the grounds was a building that had been used to cast iron for cannons and naval fittings. Once a factory, it had very high ceilings and a row of clerestory windows along the uppermost part of the walls. It was now the Biennale's Chinese Pavilion.

Just then, one of the Venice cops radioed that he'd thought he'd seen Sofia in the Pavilion. Pierre and Gerard followed their Venetian police guide as he ran toward it.

The officer outside the building said that he thought she had gone into the building.

Gerard, Pierre, and two Venice cops went in. The building was similar to the one they had just left, with disused furnaces on several sides and a high ceiling. Police were stationed at the two exits as visitors were being let out one by one. "She won't elude us this time."

Pierre was the first to notice that a number of the visitors in the crowded building were staring at the ceiling and pointing. Looking up he saw Sofia, who had scaled one of the furnaces to the top of the building, climbing out a clerestory windows. By the time the police had made their way through the crowd to the outside, there was no sign of her. Few people walked along the side of the building facing the water on the arsenal side. But two women, carrying Biennale bags and wearing large straw hats were standing there. One of the officers asked if they had seen a woman on the building wall. They said yes, that she came through the window and climbed down the rough brick exterior of the building. It was quite amazing, they said. They asked if it was some kind of performance art.

"No," said the policeman, "which way did she go?"

They pointed toward a white modernist building. Gerard consulted his Biennale map and said, "That's the Cuba Pavilion. Let's look for her there."

One of the officers pointed at a white van near the Cuba Pavillion. He said it seemed to be driving erratically.

"Sofia is in that van. Let's go!" shouted Gerard.

Inside the van, a terrified driver was trying to loosen a rope around his neck that Sofia, kneeling behind the driver's seat, held tightly. "Do as I say, or I'll strangle you. Drive toward the service entrance."

The driver looked back at her and again tried to loosen the rope. "Look where you are going," Sofia shouted in Italian as the driver braked suddenly to avoid hitting a group heading out of the Pavillion. She climbed into the front and reached over to open the driver's side door to push the driver out.

The driver was still holding on by his seat belt when Pierre reached the back of the van, grabbed the handles to the rear doors, and climbed on. He opened one door and got his footing. He took out his gun.

"Sofia, throw the keys to the van out the door or I'll shoot."

As she continued to try to loosen the driver's seat belt, Gerard ran to the driver's side of the van, reached in, and put the gear shift into park. The sudden stop jerked Sofia forward into the windshield. Moments later, two French policemen and a Venice officer pulled her out of the van and handcuffed her.

No one talked as she was hustled into a police car. It was noon.

Chapter Forty-Four

The next day, Pierre and Gerard were sitting in the command center when Terzazo entered the room.

"When can you turn Sofia over to us?" Gerard said with great satisfaction.

Terzazo was silent. He looked up at the beamed ceiling of the room and then looked out of a window. "I will be direct with you. We won't be turning her over to you. We have released her."

Gerard leaned forward. "Why, Steffani, would you do such a thing? She's a wanted criminal."

"Not in Italy," Terzazo said, a bit defensively. "At the most, we might be able to prosecute her for participation in an art fraud. Finding the killer of the Naples gangster is not a high priority for us. Good riddance. And, I have reviewed the files. All the evidence against her in that murder is circumstantial." Terzazo's tone softened. "I can understand your dismay at this decision. If I were in your place, I would feel the same way. But I will tell you something about Italy that may help you to understand the decision to release her. The greatest scourge facing our country is the potential of widespread drug use. You know what the drug epidemic has done to the social order in the United States, Mexico, and other countries."

"And art fraud is low on the list?" Pierre said, clearly irritated.

"Let me explain her release by contrasting, very broadly, your country and mine. France is a highly centralized country run out of Paris, and it has a long history as a unified nation. Italy is fragmented. It only became a political entity in the middle of the nineteenth century. The differences in economic development and wealth between Northern Italy and Southern Italy are unlike any regional differences in France.

"We have had over sixty governments and perhaps twenty-five plus prime ministers since the end of the Second World War. The role that the central government plays is not so much to govern as to manage the various local and institutional interests in the country. There are local interests—the South for example relies heavily on government subsidies. There are powerful institutions—labor unions, business interests, the Catholic Church. All must be balanced to maintain some semblance of civic order.

"As for the drug trade, one of the interests the government must take into account in its balancing act is the criminal organizations, which also are divided to some extent by the geography of the country. We cannot eradicate the drug trade. France has not been able to—the United States has not. In fact, over half of the inmates of American federal prisons are there because of drug-related crimes, and the drug trade continues unabated. Supply side interdiction efforts have not worked anywhere in the West.

"Our job as the Italian police is the security of our citizens. Since we cannot eradicate the drug business, we can, to some degree, regulate it by maintaining some type of dialogue with our Italian criminal organizations. This balance, delicate and tenuous at best cannot be maintained if non-Italian criminal organizations take root here. So, it's a high priority to keep the Mexicans, the Russians, and others at bay.

"Sofia Mostov provided us with a wealth of information—she even gave us voice recordings—on the efforts of

Francesco Perez and his colleagues to move into the drug trade in Italy. She did this in exchange for our agreement to release her.

The French policemen looked at Terzazo in amazed silence.

"I must now arrange for Perez's transfer to Rome. While I'm sure that you are not happy with the release of Sofia Mostov, I hope you understand the reasoning of my superiors. I also hope we have an opportunity to work together again. You two are fine policemen.

"If you decide to remain in Venice, Gerard, we can facilitate your stay. But, you and Pierre may want to return to Paris. While I have no information as to her next destination, a reasonable surmise is that it's Paris. Perhaps she has unfinished business there."

With that comment and a smile, Steffani Terzazo left the room. Gerard and Pierre sat silently, looking at each other.

"She seems to have eluded us again," said Pierre.

"Sofia has very well-developed survival instincts," Gerard said. "My guess is that she killed Gallet, and we should pursue that but, as is her trademark, the killer left no traces."

"Except maybe for the choice of location for the murder," said Pierre.

"If a message, a subtle one indeed," Gerard said. "Well, at least we seem to have a case against the Mexican prisoners for the Marseilles murders, and they'll probably confess in exchange for a deal. And we can keep pursuing her. I wonder what kind of trouble she and her uncle are up to in Moscow and if the Russian government has any interest in recovering the paintings that were apparently captured from the Germans."

"What do you think?" Pierre said.

"Russia is an enigma, but since I'm sure many of the works were stolen in France, perhaps the French government may follow up with the Russians. Some of these paintings may still be in Russia, others are in Italy and France, and perhaps

Montenegro. Wherever they are, they will produce a tangled web of ownership and jurisdictional claims."

"What now?"

"Now we return to France. Terzazo was not making idle conversation in his surmise that Sofia is heading for Paris."

Chapter Forty-Five

Early the same morning, Francesco Perez looked up as Sofia Mostov was led into his drab cell in the Venice Questura.

"I'm glad to see you, Sofia, but not in these circumstances. I'm sure that I can arrange my release—after all how serious can the Italians take the sale of forged art? Then I will try to get you released. Perhaps now that we have been through this, you will see the virtue of my proposal to you."

"Actually, Francesco, I have come to say goodbye. I'm leaving Italy today. I don't think you will be released for a long time. The police know about your other business activities in Italy."

"What do you mean? How can they?" Sofia was silent. "You betrayed me for your freedom, didn't you? How could you do that? After I told you of my feelings for you. How could you? How could you?" He began to sob. Then his eyes turned black as he lunged at her. "I will kill you."

"No, you won't," she said, and motioned the waiting guard to let her out.

From the other side of the bars, she looked at him and said, "You asked how I could? To you I say—how could you?"

"How could I what?"

"How could you forget KGB rule number one?"

He looked at her, "What rule?"

She said, "Trust no one. Good day, Francesco."

And she walked away as Perez slumped against the bars, his head down.

Chapter Forty-Six

"Monsey says that the Italians are now talking. They have provided details on the drug smuggling, the murder of the two Naples gangsters, and the bribing of the customs inspectors. They also have said that the Mexicans told them that they shot the three dockworkers because they were trying to get money from them to keep quiet. The Mexicans also wanted to send a message to other dockworkers to stay out of it."

"Thus the desecration of the corpses. Well, Pierre, that's good news. When Monsey has what he needs, it's agreeable to me that he extradite the Italians. I'll tell Terzazo."

"How do you feel about Terzazo?"

Gerard got up from behind his desk and walked to the window and looked out at Notre Dame, then he said, "He's calculating and certainly doesn't put all his cards on the table. But I think he and I both share a devotion to our countries. Law enforcement in France is carried out under different assumptions than in Italy. He obviously has many sources of information. He didn't rely only on what Sofia Mostov gave him to snare Perez. He told me that they arrested two accomplices of Perez at the Rome airport trying to leave the country. I would work with him again—but my eyes would be open wider."

"He reminds me, Gerard, of Holmes in *The Adventure of the Second Stain.*"

"Abou, your Sherlock Holmes scholarship has surpassed mine. What do you mean?"

"Oh, the plot revolved around an incriminating letter that went missing. At the conclusion, it's found, mysteriously back in its original box. Asked by an English statesman who would have been compromised by the release of the letter how it got back to the box, Holmes said, 'We also have our diplomatic secrets.' Terzazo is as much a politician as a police officer."

"You're right, Pierre. But he has no choice. Thankfully, we do. And his diplomatic vocation is apparently the reason, as he told me, that the Italian government is agreeing to a request from an agency of the Russian government, that he did not name, that the paintings in Perez's gallery be returned to Moscow. When I expressed a muted surprise, he pointed out that none of them originated in Italy. I think he's glad to be rid of the paintings."

"Well, boss, what do we do now?"

Gerard slumped in his desk chair. "If Sofia has returned to Paris, we try to apprehend her. Sofia and her uncle, who is surely involved in this, will see Libidoux as the weak link. She undoubtedly killed Gallet. But Libidoux is much more of a threat to them. We will keep a close eye on him. He may well lead us to her and to Boris Vorishilov."

"Boss, you look tired."

"Pierre, I am an aging detective. I do this work because I find it interesting and because I love this country and want to serve it. I am cynical enough to know that at the levels we operate, compromises have to be made. Terzazo made one. I would have found it difficult to do what he did. But faced with his choice, I'm not sure what my decision would have been."

He then got up and walked over to the window overlooking Notre Dame.

Chapter Forty-Seven

Marc Libidoux walked into the darkened Palais Royale from the Rue Saint-Honoré. Under one of the arcades he stopped in front of a shuttered shop that sold antique toy soldiers. Out of the doorway next to the shop stepped Sofia Mostov, wearing a long black coat with a hood over her hair which was a shade of dark brown, her make-up made her look twenty-years older.

"You startled me. I almost didn't recognize you with your altered appearance."

"Did you follow my instructions?"

"Yes. Yes. I went to the reception across the street at the Le Louvre des Antiquaires moved through the crowd and took off my light-colored trench coat and left it in one of the bathrooms. Then I exited a staff entrance, quickly crossed the street, and came here. I am sure that I lost the cop who you pointed out was following me."

"Good work. You are shivering in this damp without your coat. Come closer to me."

As he huddled against Sofia, Libidoux felt a jab in his neck and reached up just as Sofia pulled a large hypodermic needle out of his neck.

"What? What are you doing?" he gasped as he felt his neck.

"I'm giving you a heart attack," Sofia said as Libidoux slumped to the ground.

Chapter Forty-Eight

PARIS

At its northeast corner, where Rue Vivienne intersects with Rue Colbert, the large building housing the Bibliothèque Nationale is built almost to the corner. Sofia walked under the cover of the Palais Royale arcades and crossed the Rue Vivienne where Boris was waiting for her in the shadow of one of the entrances to the darkened library. The rain had increased in intensity.

"Is it done?" he asked.

"Yes, it was necessary. He was starting to crack." Standing and looking up and down the street, Sofia said, "Something doesn't feel right. This street should be busy, but there are no cars."

"Or pedestrians," said Boris. "There is also a siren over at the Palais Royale. Do you think they could have found Libidoux so soon?"

"I left him lying in a darkened arcade. Someone could walk right past him and not see him."

"Unless they were following him," Boris said.

"Or me."

"*Plemyanitsa* your instincts have always been superb. A sixth sense we used to say. And you are right. There should be traffic on Petits Champs, heading toward L'Opera as well as heading up the rue Vivienne. I will keep walking up the rue Vivienne. If they are after us, that is where they will probably make their move. There would be nowhere for us to run. You take my umbrella, it will shield you from this rain and the surveillance cameras and work your way around the building staying in the shadows. You should be able to find a bus and make it to the safe house. I will call you on your burner phone. If you don't hear from me…."

Sofia hugged Boris. He couldn't tell if it was the rain or tears. He had never seen her cry. He headed up the street.

Before he even reached the corner, a stocky figure accompanied by three uniformed police officers wearing rain capes over their uniforms, walked around the corner and stepped in front of him.

Pierre Abou said, "Boris Voroshilov, you are under arrest."

Chapter Forty-Nine

As Gerard and Pierre left the ornate conference room in the headquarters of the French National Police, Pierre said, "That was nice recognition of the team. After all, we solved five murders, interrupted a drug smuggling plot in Marseilles as well as a scheme to distribute drugs in Italy and, probably eventually in France, stopped an audacious plan to sell forged art as well as to launder money, and we arrested Boris Vorishilov."

Gerard frowned slightly. "The only thing we didn't do is to put Sofia Mostov behind bars. And she has added two murders, Gallet and Libidoux, to her résumé. We have not seen the last of her and she has not seen the last of us. As for the reception, it was fine except they could have served better champagne. I talked to Terzazo this morning to thank him for the very positive letter he sent to applaud our work. He seems pleased with the outcome. He has Perez locked up, although the Italian government is getting some pressure to extradite him to Mexico. Steffano says that he won't be extradited."

Gerard's tone became less sure, almost shy, "Pierre, I have something not related to police business that I need your advice on. I am on vacation as of now, and so are you, so let's walk across the river to the Hemingway Bar and have some excellent champagne."

Once inside, Pierre stretched his legs out in the small, richly paneled room just off the Rue Cambon entrance to the

Ritz hotel. "Thank you, Gerard, this is a treat. Did Hemingway actually drink here?"

"Yes, although he drank everywhere in Paris."

"Let me also thank you, Gerard, for the extra two weeks of vacation. It was a surprise and a pleasant one."

"You earned it and more," said Gerard. "Will you stay in Paris?"

"I'm going to take my wife to Marseilles for part of the time. We can both visit family and," he said with a wink, "I will drop by Marseilles Police Headquarters and see if Monsey needs any help. Maybe I will bring Sherlock Holmes with me."

Gerard smiled. "Maybe I should accompany you to Marseilles. With you, Holmes, and me helping him, Monsey may decide to take early retirement!"

Pierre said, "Where will you be going?"

"That's why I need your advice. I'm planning to accompany Catherine to the States. She has meetings in New York and I'm going to suggest that we also go to Wisconsin to visit her family."

"Sounds like a great trip. But what do you need my advice on?"

"I'm going to propose to Catherine, and I can't decide where to do it."

Pierre raised his champagne glass. "I'm not surprised. I'm very happy for you. She's a wonderful woman. Have you thought about the logistics? Will the two of you live in Paris?"

"You have the mind of a very good cop. I had never thought of the question of where we would live as a matter of *logistics*. What is important to me is that I love her. Where we live is secondary. But I don't even know if she will say yes."

"Boss, you are more of a romantic than I ever would have thought. Why don't you propose to her at Grand Vefour. You both love that restaurant."

"It's too public. I need a place that's private. Where did

you propose to Helene? And please don't say on your father's fishing boat."

"Actually, I thought about that, but I got down on my knee in her family's living room. Why don't you take her for a moonlight stroll through the Palais Royale, sit on one of those old benches and ask here there? If she says yes, take her to dinner at Vefour. If she says no, take her there anyway, just don't order champagne. Do you have a ring?"

"I have my mother's engagement ring. My sister sent it to me, and I snuck one of Catherine's rings out and brought both of them to my jeweler to get the right size. He delivered it this morning. I will show it to you." Gerard took a ring box, opened it and showed it to Pierre.

"She will say yes."

• • •

The next evening, Gerard and Catherine strolled arm in arm past the Louvre and across the Rue Rivoli to the Rue St. Honoré.

"Gerard, this is a beautiful spring evening for a walk, but do you have a destination in mind?"

"I do. Let's walk into the Palais Royale. Wonderful spring flower aromas, benches to sit on."

A few minutes later they sat in the gardens as the evening slowly faded into a soft Paris spring night.

"As I told you Catherine, the department is very pleased with the completion of the case. Again thank you for your help."

"You are welcome. All I did was save Larson & McTabbit from a messy claim on the art Libidoux wanted to insure. But now I must go to New York for management meetings and to decide on the next steps for the Paris office."

Gerard hesitated, then said, "If it's agreeable with you, my dear, I would like to accompany you to New York."

"Why Gerard, I would love it if you came to New York with me."

"We could also go to Wisconsin."

"You must miss my mom's country stew."

"I do indeed. And there's something I must discuss with your father."

"My father!" Catherine looked at him, surprised. "What on earth do you want to discuss with him?"

Gerard turned to face her and reached into the pocket of his suit jacket. "What I would like to say to him is that you and I have decided to get married and that I would like his approval."

Catherine gasped as Gerard opened a ring box and placed a ring on Catherine's finger. "I love you. Will you marry me?"

After looking into his eyes for a moment, Catherine said, "oui, mon amour." They kissed.

"This ring is beautiful and it fits my finger perfectly. Gerard it takes my breath away."

"The ring was my mother's. My sister wanted you to have it. I have to admit that I took a chance and borrowed one of your rings for sizing."

Catherine kissed him again and said, "I don't think I have seen a diamond this large and yet so well balanced in its setting. And the emerald cut is my favorite—and set off with sapphire baguettes. I can't stop looking at it." She smiled, "I can hardly wait for my next college reunion."

Laughing and kissing her, Gerard said, "Let's go next door to Vefour for dinner. This calls for a very special champagne."

"Will we sit at our favorite table?"

"Of course. Maybe we'll get our own plaque."

Author's Note

The Russian Collector is a work of fiction. All the names, characters, incidents, and places in the novel are the products of my imagination or are used fictitiously.

The artists mentioned in the novel are historical figures except for Ilia Dilinov and Anton Yevgeny. I imagined them. There are no Dilinov paintings in the Tretyakov in Moscow, the Museum of Modern Art in New York or the D'Orsay in Paris.

There are many books and articles on the subject of art forgery. There seems to be an arms race among forgers, such as more sophisticated techniques to fake old paint on paintings or glazes on ancient pottery. Some of the sources I consulted include: *The Art Forger's Handbook* by Eric Hebborn, *The Man Who Made Vermeers*, by Jonathan Lopez, *Provenance* by Laney Salisbury and Aly Sujo and *False Impressions* by Thomas Hoving.

B. A. Shapiro's novel, *The Art Forger*, takes the reader through in detail a fictional artist's attempt to create a fake.

Sergei Androyov must have consulted many of the available sources to perfect his technique. He also probably read the article in the October 28, 2013 issue of *The New York Times* by Barboza, Bowley and Cox, *Forging an Art Market in China*.

The havoc wreaked on the art world by the Nazi theft of so much of Europe's art is a subject that continues to unfold as more dimensions of this tragic episode are revealed. In addition to many newspaper and magazine articles and other books, *The Lost Museum*, by Hector Feliciano, *The Faustian Bargain* by Jonathan Petropoulos, *The Linz File: Hitler's Plunder of Europe's Art* by Charles de Jaeger were helpful sources as was *The Monuments Men* by Robert Edsel.

The disputes over art seized by the Red Army at the end of World War II also continues to rage on. I found *Beautiful Loot; The Soviet Plunder of Europe's Art Treasures* by Konstantin Akinsha and Grigorii Kozlov helpful background.

You will not find Boris's dacha outside of Moscow, or Sidney Pebbles auction house in Paris. Marc Libidoux's gallery in Paris and the Galerie Perez in Venice are also fictional creations.

Most of the restaurants in Paris, Venice and Milan described in the book as well as their locations are amalgams of actual establishments. Le Grand Véfour is a real and distinguished restaurant and the place where the romance between Gerard and Catherine began in my novel, *The Last Layer*, so of course they had to dine there again.

The French National Police have their headquarters in the Ministry of the Interior building in Paris's Eight Arrondissement near the Élysée Palace. I decided to move the headquarters to the building on the Île de la Cité so they could co-locate with the Prefecture of Police of Paris and provide Gerard an office convenient to his apartment on the Île Saint-Louis. Who could not dream of walking to work each day from the Île Saint-Louis and around Notre Dame.

Acknowledgments

Many thanks to my friends and family who encouraged me to write this second book.

Special thanks to Jim Carona, gallerist extraordinaire of the Heather James galleries, for reading an early draft. To the extent I took his advice the book is better; to the extent that I did not, the responsibility is mine. The same is true for others that I consulted. You know who you are.

Nick Dimassis of Forty Press is a superb editor, knowledgeable, insightful and supportive. Quite a package. His colleague Kelly Keady made a major editing contribution. No one will ever accuse him of beating around the bush. Also thanks to Forty Press's Joe Riley for his publishing skill and to John Toren for his cover design.

My long-time assistant, the now retired Sue Seals, prepared the early drafts of the manuscript. Josh Miller guided me through the intricacies of using the Word program.

Finally, last but far from least, my wife Linda supported me and endured the trials of living with an author.